T0165308

THE MOON OF TWILIGHT

CARL F. ROBINSON

THE MOON OF TWILIGHT

iUniverse books may be ordered through booksellers or by contacting:

iUniverse
1663 Liberty Drive
Bloomington, IN 47403
www.iuniverse.com
1-800-Authors (1-800-288-4677)

ISBN: 978-1-4917-6955-3 (sc)
ISBN: 978-1-4917-6956-0 (e)

Library of Congress Control Number: 2015908828

Print information available on the last page.

iUniverse rev. date: 06/08/2015

Contents

Chapter 1

BOREAS: PLANET OF THE TWILIGHT

"No, it is not a good idea to borrow money to buy breeding stock from Santa Fe," said Gladys calmly but in a very firm voice. Her eyes didn't meet her son Harold's. Instead she continued to busy herself by mixing sourdough starter with flour.

Gladys was wearing a plain gray dress with a blue apron. Her eyes were green, and her brown hair was beginning to get streaks of gray. She continued, "I'm not going to lend you the money because I don't have any to spare, and no bank on Illissos will lend to a child."

The word *child* hit Harold like an iron fist. He could feel a hot, angry flush gather on his cheeks, but then he realized that the older men didn't seem to lose their tempers around their women, and he decided to clamp down on the feeling.

Gladys continued, "I know that you want to expand our stock of cattle, and I know you wish to use any profits on the cattle to buy a Cossack sword from New Lydia. But if you wait until you're eighteen, a sword will be issued to you when you join the militia. You're not eighteen yet, and the way I see it, I'm still the protector of all my children. The militia doesn't need my oldest kid just yet, and you're still too young to go chasing Bavianer on your own."

Harold's anger returned, but he just managed to repress its heat, and before Harold could respond, his mother continued. "The adult world is pretty tough. All adult ventures have a way of veering into unexpected difficulty. Also, borrowing money to expand the herd might not be a way to get ahead. The calves could take sick or get eaten by a Bavianer, or the price of beef could fall below what you borrowed, and you'd still be in debt after the animals go to market. It is best to let things grow naturally. Don't rush. When you are really an adult, not only will you know, but everyone else will too."

Harold wanted to reply. He wanted to say the pasture grass had expanded several acres so they could increase the herd without needing to buy more feed. He wanted to say he was the man of the house and put in a man's work, and he should get a man's respect. He wanted to say that taking risks was what brought rewards. But his irritation at being called a child and hearing a no to his plan took over, and he could only manage a frustrated sigh. Harold could feel through the anger that his mother was saying something rational, but he felt ready for the challenges of adulthood. He especially wanted to cut down a Bavianer with a sword, if only to avenge his father. He did his best to not explode with tearful rage, choked out an "okay" to his mother, and walked out of the well-lit house to the gathering blue twilight gloom outside.

He just needed to cool off—walk around a bit. Harold looked around the farmstead. He recalled the lines of a song his mother used to sing to him:

Twilight.
Blue twilight.
Blue gloom; blue sky; and dark, shadowed ground.

On Illissos, everyone knew the sayings about the blue twilight. "There is danger in the blue. It's best to carry a light. Stay within the light. Keep off the gloom."

And then there were the sayings that rhymed. "There's doom in the gloom. It's right when it's bright. Always fight in the light."

This twilight and the sayings about it were the result of the unique place Illissos inhabited and the unique people who lived on it. Illissos was a moon. It was one of twenty-one moons orbiting a gas giant planet named Boreas. The only moon of the twenty-one that supported life, Illissos was tidally locked with Boreas. Therefore, the same side of the moon constantly faced Boreas, while at the same time, Illissos orbited the great planet. A single spin around Boreas was what the human settlers of Illissos called an Orbweek.

A single Orbweek was divided into four different days with four different light conditions. The days were named after the light conditions: Fullday, when the light from the sun shined upon Illissos, was just like day on Earth. Fullday was followed by Descent. During Descent, the sun was at the horizon and progressively going down. The light conditions at this time are more like those of twilight on Earth. The sun shone like a spotlight on the western horizon for a time, and then the rays peeked weakly over the horizon until darkness fully fell. Once the sun was out of the picture, it was Fulldark. Here, Boreas shone down on Illissos with a gloomy blue light, and the stars could be seen. The last day of an Orbweek was Ascent, which was the opposite of Descent. Throughout Ascent, the sun slowly rose. Each day was ten hours long, and the people of Illissos slept during Ascent and Descent. It was best to sleep during those times because one could get two full working days during Fullday and Fulldark. In the cities, the people used artificial light to help them see, and most farmers adjusted their activities so that they would spend their working Fulldark hours near some source of light.

Midway from the house to the barn, Harold looked at the darkening Illissos sky. It was nearly Fulldark. Boreas glowed with a soft blue light. Perkunas and Potrimpo, the two moons that could be seen from the side of Illissos where Harold lived, continued on their short orbits around Boreas. Perkunas was the same beige color as Illissos. Potrimpo was gray. The view of the sky from a farmhouse on Illissos was a dazzling sight. In one sweep of the eye, an Illissosan could take in the glory and splendor of the universe.

Harold looked at the vast heavens and then down toward the garden where he spent so much time growing as many green vegetables as he could. The moon of Illissos was in the habitable zone of its star and was fortunate in that it orbited Boreas fast enough to allow the whole of the moon to get enough heat for liquid water. Boreas itself also reflected solar heat. On the lowlands of Illissos, it never got below freezing, but it also never became too hot. With the low levels of light and the constant cool temperatures, all plants on Illissos needed genetic modification to grow. Of course, the poles were icy. The mountains were also cold, and some held glaciers at the higher altitudes. Often, clouds would shroud the mountains, and when the clouds lifted, they'd be covered in a glaze of snow and ice.

Harold was fifteen in Earth years this year. His cheeks were just starting to get the stubble of facial hair. Curly brown wisps extended from his sideburns past his ears. In a few more months, or perhaps a year, Harold would have a decent enough beard, and it would be ritually shaven by a priest in front of his family and friends, and Harold would be admitted into full fellowship of the religion of Illissos. He would be permitted to wear the Cap of Faith, a conical wool cap with the top pulled forward during religious holidays and worship services. If he wanted, he could wear the cap all the time. Some Illissos settlers did, but only the most pious.

Harold wasn't sure what to make of the Cap of Faith. Most of the men he admired didn't wear them unless they were attending a particular ceremony.

When the first stubble started to appear on his face, Harold had decided to put away childish things and take to manhood early. He'd appealed to one of the priests in Hattusa to shave him early, but the priest had begged off, insisting his mother needed to agree to the idea. His mother had not gone in on this plan, and she continued to treat him like a child.

The priests on Illissos, the shaving rituals, and the Cap of Faith were all part of the peculiar religion that had given rise to the human settlement on Illissos. The settlers were a group of religious dissenters from Earth. The religion's founder was an Englishman with the impossibly plain name of Thomas Budd. One day, Budd was hiking across Pendle Hill, a flattop rise in the north of England. During his walk, he was knocked to the ground and held by the throat by an unseen force. The force explained to Budd that it was the combined force of the ancient gods of all humanity. These gods were tasking him to create again a viable following, which would restore their position in the spiritual world and bring about salvation for the elect of humanity.

Budd then changed his name to the Great Dissenter, and his religion became known as the Ancient Faith—so called because the religion involved worship of the combined form of the ancient gods. The Great Dissenter went down from Pendle Hill and began to preach that very day, and that very day he was thrown in prison for disorderly conduct. Upon his release, he returned to Pendle Hill to receive further instructions from the powerful force. The Great Dissenter called this force the Voice of the Gods. Over the next year, he received inspiration to write the Scriptures of the Ancient Faith.

After publishing his scriptures, he gained a following. He appointed his most talented followers as priests and put them in charge of the growing community.

This new religion, the Ancient Faith, served its adherents well. The scriptures helped answer the fundamental spiritual questions of humanity. Additionally, the ancient gods of all humanity spoke to the early dissenters all the time. Miracles were performed, visions were seen, and the new converts moved and worked with great determination to change the world. However, not all of humanity accepted the Ancient Faith. The people who tended to take to the Ancient Faith came mostly from Europe or North America. Even in those areas, skeptics scoffed at the new scripture and held it to be a forgery. Many were uncomfortable with a group claiming to be a holy elect living within their midst.

After several bombings of houses of worship for members of the Ancient Faith, the Great Dissenter and those of the Ancient Faith fled England to an abandoned mining town in northern New Mexico. There they came again in conflict with the locals, only in a more terrible way. Their settlement was attacked many times by a large armed force called the Española Marrones. Many of the faithful were killed. With such pressure against the faithful and their leader mounting, The Great Dissenter gathered all the supplies, tools, books, and other items necessary to start a civilization and took his followers to the spaceport at Jornada del Muerto, New Mexico. From there, they passed through the star-portal to make their stand on Illissos.

After moving to Illissos, the settlers sometimes call their belief system the Ancient Faith of Illissos, but as is true for all people who take on a form of group identity, those of Illissos had several different ways of referring to themselves. Sometimes they were settlers; other times, humans, Earthmen, or people of the Ancient Faith. And sometimes Illissosans identified with the city in which they lived.

Harold took his mind off the founding and history of the colony on Illissos when he approached one of the irrigation stations. Harold stopped his aimless, cooling-off walk and inspected the sprinkler system that watered the garden. Illissos had water, but rain was not always forthcoming. The moon was a semiarid environment. Without the water, the crops didn't grow.

Suddenly, Harold heard a noise. He shone a small light clipped to his shirt toward the noise but saw nothing. All Illissosans carried small lights clipped to a buttonhole on their shirts. It helped during the long stretches of gloomy twilight.

So much darkness on Illissos. So much fear in the twilight.

The humans of Illissos had all those sayings about danger in the twilight because Illissos was host to a creature called Bavianer. The Bavianer were dark, hairy, primate-like creatures with what space settlers called near-human intelligence. They only had near-human intelligence, though. This designation of "near-human intelligence" meant that, under religious law, Bavianer occupied a gray area of theology. They were possibly a species that could be termed "sentient beings" under religious law. Such a designation by the religious courts meant that Bavianer became accountable to the gods of all humanity for salvation. For now, the issue remained officially undecided by the religious authorities. Most of those who lived near Hattusa believed the Bavianer did not have moral sense. To put it a different way, the Bavianer were smart, but they didn't practice any theology, toolmaking, or noninstinctive construction. Thus, they were animals—very dangerous animals.

Harold shone the small light again around the darkened perimeter of the farm. His beam lingered on a salt lick. Sometimes the creatures liked the salt, enough that they fought over it. This time there was nothing, but Harold had a feeling. It was a feeling of rising dread—the sort of uncomfortable feeling a person on Earth has when the weather turns from a warm spring rain to the sudden, unsettling, tornado-on-the way coldness. His skin crawled, and every noise and shadow seemed ominous.

He shone the light to his left, away from the barn. Its beam illuminated the genetically modified pasture grass that the domestic animals used for grazing and then out toward the native Illissos scrub. The light scattered there, and Harold could see nothing. No Bavianer. But the feeling didn't go away.

Then traveling on the wind was the faint order of the Bavianer. Its smell was a chemical order, not unlike the waves of toxic fumes from an oil refinery. This smell meant one thing—a swarming mass of the creatures.

Harold returned to the farmhouse, his heart in his throat. His mother and his two blonde sisters, Nellie and Naomi, were hurriedly collecting their grab-and-go bags. Nellie, the oldest of his younger sisters, announced that Mayor Winchurst of Hattusa had declared a state of emergency. The message had come on the comms device from the Hattusa comms center. All outer farmsteads were to be secured, and the people and their most important domestic animals were to retreat to their preassigned garrison house and livery stable.

Harold's family had been through this before and had drilled to ensure they could quickly make a getaway. Nonetheless, Harold had to look at his hands and feet and *will* them to go to the barn and get the camels ready. Harold grabbed the camels from the corral, walked them with a leader rope past the stock of preserved food in the barn to the tack room, where he saddled Clem, his favorite brown-eyed riding camel, and two others, Bedouin Bit and King Faisal. Harold couldn't help but think of the Zeppelins of New Lydia. A recent news article had discussed their arrival on Illissos. These great crafts operated on antigravity, and the plan was to use them to fly to the different moons of Boreas and support mining operations. A Zeppelin was perfect for this—it didn't need to get to the space between the moons of Boreas by means of rocket propulsion, and on the airless moons, it could fly without needing air to run across a wing to provide lift like with an airplane. Once back in New Lydia, the minerals could be sent through the star-portal in exchange for goods from Earth.

Oh for a ride on a Zeppelin right now, thought Harold.

Aside from rail service between Santa Fe and New Lydia and the Zeppelins, modern transportation on Illissos was in want. Harold had heard of cars and trucks and flying craft such as helicopters, but on the far frontier, spare parts were impossible to come by for regular people and large-scale manufacturing was nonexistent. Complex and high-end finished goods from Earth, which rarely passed through the portal, were too expensive for most people—especially those of Hattusa. Additionally, there were few roads, mostly just dirt trails. On the few times it rained, those trails would be too muddy and impassable for anything but an expensive off-road vehicle specially imported from Earth with a trailer-load of spare parts. On the other hand, beasts of burden were perfect for the local conditions.

Harold struggled to get the camels ready; every second counted during a Bavianer swarm. Shane, a fellow classmate, had shown him pictures of victims from an earlier swarm, and the bloodied corpses had haunted his dreams for six Orbweeks.

When the last saddle was cinched tight on King Faisal, Harold helped his mother get the girls on the camels, and off they went.

Harold kept his rifle in hand the whole way to Hattusa, all while scanning every bush and shrub and patch of long grass for Bavianer. His sisters helped him by shining their flashlights to the left and right of the road. Despite holding a rifle and riding a camel, Harold was at a bit of a disadvantage without a sword. Shooting a rifle from the back of a camel is a very difficult thing to do. The rider can accidently shoot the camel's head, and it is nearly impossible to aim with the camel plodding along. Additionally the loud bang of the rifle caused most camels to jump. No, a Cossack-style shaska saber was perfect for use while mounted. His father had had a sword, but it had disappeared after he died. Either the militia had taken it back to the armory for use by another soldier, or it had been lost on the field. Harold had never gotten an answer as to the final status of the sword.

As Harold and his family closed the distance to Hattusa, other families of refugees arrived. Some were on camels, some came with horses, and others had mules and donkeys. A shepherd with several collie dogs and a flock of fifty sheep snarled traffic in front of the city gates. The gate was a mix of cries and bellows from the farm animals, shouts from people, and flashlight beams probing everywhere.

"Keep 'em moving now!" shouted an older man with a militia uniform.

The walls of Hattusa were made from adobe. Blockhouses with firing platforms were positioned in key areas to allow defenders to fire upon Bavianer as necessary. Within the city, the houses were likewise made of adobe brick. Harold's family moved toward their garrison house, where they would find shelter for themselves and the camels.

The garrison house was the same one that they'd stayed in during the last Bavianer swarm two years earlier, and it's sameness made Harold think back to that day two years ago when he'd gotten off Clem, legs wobbling.

***

A mob of girls, tweens mostly, swarmed past him toward Nellie and Naomi. Each girl let out a high-pitched giggle, and their combined laughter made a sort of feminine, girlish roar. His sisters squealed with delight. Safely arriving in town after the scary journey following a Bavianer warning always brought great happiness to the tween girls. The girls had been promised a shopping trip downtown to help kill the time while the men were off hunting the creatures and protecting the city.

Harold pushed past the girls. He spotted his father leaning over his mom for a quick kiss. "I'll be back soon, love," his dad said.

His mother replied with a quick, "Best be."

Without a speaking further, his father turned and headed toward the armory. The other men were also making quick departures.

Suddenly, a thin, hollow-faced woman with a limp and a small child spoke to his mother, "Gladys, is that a new dress?" Mrs. Parker was a farmwife from the northern side of Hattusa.

His mother looked at the dress and then tugged at it with both of her hands. "This old thing—no I've had it for a while, but I've not yet worn it to the garrison house." She then added, with a twinkle in her eyes. "I made it myself."

Harold couldn't believe that his mother and Mrs. Parker could stand around and talk about dresses when there was so much excitement. A great Bavianer hunt was on. Harold didn't want to spend the time cooped up with the women and children. He ran toward his father and grabbed him by the sleeve. "Dad, hold on!"

His father turned, and his lips turned into a faint smile. "No, son," he said. "You can't come along. I need you to help your mother and look after your sisters."

"I don't want to be a babysitter," replied Harold. "I want to help you."

His father then looked at him with a sadness he'd never seen before, and he said, "When you're needed for this, you'll be called, and you won't have an option to keep away." His father then turned away and headed for the armory.

***

That was the last time Harold had spoken to his father. He had been killed during that very Bavianer swarm. Harold shook off the memory and moved to take the camels to the stables. Just as before, the men were busy dropping off their families and heading to the armory. The women hugged as they reunited. Harold looked at his sisters. They wore expressions that mixed the sorrowful reminder of the loss of their father with relief at arriving safely. His mother's face was expressionless, but her eyes looked through the garrison house to something far, far off. She looked exhausted. It was now Ascent, and the hours normally spent sleeping would be consumed by preparations for survival during the siege. The men would spend the time getting ready for the counterattack. Harold knew most of the refugees would try and get *some* sleep, but he wouldn't be able to. His very blood pulsed with energy and excitement.

One of the men dropping off his family already had his militia uniform on. It had three stripes on his sleeve denoting that he was a sergeant. Harold went to him and said, "I want to join up."

"How old are you?" the sergeant asked.

"I'm fifteen," replied Harold. "I'm the man of my house so to speak and have been here on the frontier nearly my whole life. I know how to work a gun and can ride too. I'm tired of holding up in town with the kids while the grown-ups get the fun on a Bavianer chase."

"Hold on," said the sergeant. "These Bavianer chases, as you call them, can get pretty dangerous. It's not as bad as when Hattusa was first chartered, but every contest is uncertain. We'll win this one of course, but it will be uncertain at the individual level. You remember that Bavianer swarm two years back? A man in the militia lost his leg, and other militiamen were killed. I'm sure they'll still be some Bavianer around when you're eighteen."

With that statement, the sergeant picked up his kit and headed to the armory. Harold noticed how he carried the sheathed Cossack-style sword. He didn't have it hung around his waist but instead held the weapon from the middle of the scabbard in his left hand, in a way that expressed a cool confidence in its razor-sharp, steel edge. His body posture was calm and aloof. It was very impressive.

Harold stopped him again. "My father was one of the men killed. I want to avenge him. I wish to help out and not hang around here."

The sergeant looked at him again. He had crow's feet on his eyes and a lean, muscular frame. "Tell you what," he said in a voice that was mildly approving, "do you have a comms device?"

"My family does," replied Harold.

The sergeant continued, "All right, my name is Anthony Burbeen. I'll send you a message—give you an update when things turn around. Perhaps I'll even get you out of the city once we've broken the back of the besieging force and have 'em on the run. If we soften them up, it may be all right for you to come and help out." After exchanging comms device details with Harold, the sergeant turned and continued to the armory.

More people were coming and going around the garrison house. A bearded man in a cloak walked by and showed a piece of paper to the garrison house leader and was let inside. A kid leaned against the wall. It was Francis; Harold remembered him from the last Bavianer swarm and siege. He would be eleven now, thought Harold. Francis had sandy brown hair and freckles.

"They wouldn't take ya?" asked Francis.

"Nope," said Harold, irritated that this kid would ask such a question.

"My dad is in the militia," continued Francis. "He says the Bavianer are pretty tough. But even though they're tough, one day the Bavianer will go the way of the dodo bird. It's only a matter of time before we drive them out."

Harold didn't like that idea. How could he prove himself if there were no enemies to fight when he came of age? "I suppose you're correct. I guess that's why I feel like I need to join up this go-round," replied Harold. "I feel that I'm ready for the challenge of this conflict. I'd like to do my bit. I'd like to be a man. I think there is still a way."

"A way to do what?" Francis asked.

"To join up," answered Harold. "To do something to lift the siege," he added.

Francis let out a chuckle. "You could wait three more years." But then his face showed a surprising sympathy. He continued, "I know how you feel."

Harold continued to be irritated from the militia brush-off but was pleased he might get to go out once the battle turned to their favor. Since it was Ascent and since he'd successfully secured a chance to do glory this siege, Harold returned to his family's sleeping area and fell asleep.

At the dawn of Fullday, Harold and his family, along with Francis and the other refugees from the garrison house, made their way to the town commons to watch the militia gather. On the way to the commons, Harold thought about what to do when he got the message to join the militia on the comms device. He'd take his rifle and Clem, but what about a sword? Could he get one from one of the men in the militia? Could he borrow one?

The refugees and townspeople gathered at the commons. The commons consisted of a manicured grassy field, which held a portico. To the front of the portico was a stone structure that held the sacred fire, which was lit during important community events. The fire was burning brightly. In the center of the commons was the sacred stone circle, which was used during ceremonies of the Ancient Faith and occasionally decorated to highlight some holy day or important religious concept. On the far side of the field was the Hattusa mayor's residence. Mayor Winchurst was on the portico along with the other authorities from the city government. He was wearing a russet coat with a ruffled shirt. The coat appeared to be the delicate felt worn by all high-class people. Laborers, farmers, and working folk wore clothes with a twill weave. The mayor's face appeared calm.

To the right of the mayor was Bogedet, the High Priestess of Hattusa. She wore the red robe of the Ancient Faith and had a white sash. The white sash indicated that she was a priestess in charge of other priests and priestesses. All priests or priestesses were required to change their name to one of the sacred names described by the Great Dissenter in the scriptures. The priests' red garb marked an incident that arose during the conflict with the Española Marrones. The Great Dissenter had decreed after a particularly bad attack that all priests would wear red so that both friend and foe could easily know who the leaders of the true followers of the gods of all humanity were and be inspired or terrorized depending on who was who. After this change in dress, the Espanola Marrones had attacked again, but the Great Dissenter and his priests had organized his followers for defense. During the attack, the red-robed priests had gone out among the defenders and inspired a vicious, heroic response to the Morrones' attack. Badly hurt, the Española Marrones were thus unable to stop those of the Ancient Faith from heading toward the spaceport without being robbed.

The militia was gathered into three companies, and the men stood at attention facing the portico. The commander of the militia, Colonel Caleb Shreve, brought the men to parade rest. Harold couldn't help but look at the formation of soldiers with a fascinated envy. The men had their Cossack swords safely sheathed and their carbine rifles slung across their back. The carbines had a folding stock to make them as easy to carry while on horseback. The carbines were only held at the ready when the men were dismounted or in camp somewhere.

Mayor Winchurst moved to the podium to address the militia and gathered civilians. "Today, our frontier settlement is once again under threat from the scourge of the Bavianer. They have attacked a farmstead upriver from Hattusa and killed several people. Reports have arrived that a large swarm of the beasts have moved to the heights above the Mighty River. As usual in such cases, I've directed the rural residents of the area to come to the safety of our town's stout walls.

"Today, good citizens, our militia is called and assembled here to rid us of this threat. They will sally forth and do battle against this foe. Reports of our foe's numbers and disposition are such that we believe they will crumble at our first charge. Nonetheless, this will be a difficult time. This administration has prepared for a Bavianer siege. Your tax money and fees have gone to support the garrison house and equip the militia, and a good portion of this year's produce has been stored, canned, and preserved. Our engineers, plumbers, electricians, and townspeople have turned what was once a barren Illissos hill next to the Mighty River into a bastion of civilization, where we can follow our religion, raise our families, and more fully secure the fruits of our labor with security.

"Arise, mighty militia, and destroy our enemies. May you wield the sword with great courage and great skill, and may your shots always strike true. Hattusa! We shall not falter; we shall not fail."

Then the priestess moved to the podium. She outstretched her arms to the sky in the same pose that *The Great Dissenter* had taken on the day of the final battle in New Mexico. She began to speak. "Gods of All Humanity, protect our militia.

May we find justice in the coming battle!" Then she threw sacrificial incense into the sacred fire. Instantly, the air filled with a sticky sweat smell that turned Harold's stomach. A great puff of white smoke rose from the sacred fire, but then a breeze kicked up, and the smoke vanished in an instant.

Colonel Shreve gave some commands; Harold's ears honed in on the crisp words. He wanted to know what was said and how to recognize the colonel's voice. When he got the word to leave the city and help out, he'd need to know what his commander's voice sounded like and what his commands might be. A good soldier followed orders.

The militia marched to the armory to make their final preparations to ride out against the Bavianer. As the sun crept up, the Bavianer became groggy. The militia would mount horses and head out, equipped with their Cossack swords and carbines, and ride down the Bavianer. It had always happened this way. The first settlers of New Lydia had learned this technique through hard trial and error in the early days and had swept the creatures from the surrounding area. Santa Fe had also done the same thing, only later.

Fullday was upon Hattusa. The militia divided into two parts. The first provided the guard for the town and the logistical support, and the greater part headed out on horseback through the main gate. The men looked superb with their sabers shining. The town cheered their departure. Harold's sisters—and Francis—yelled themselves hoarse as the horsemen went by. Harold did not cheer; instead, he thought about what to do when the call came to go help out.

Chapter 2

SETTLING IN TO SIEGE

Once the militia left, quiet came upon the city. The crowd began to mill around. Those who lived in town returned to their normal houses, and the refugee families returned to their garrison houses. A militia captain with a prosthetic leg ordered the gate closed, and two gray-haired men, each with only a single stripe for rank on his tunic, closed the door and took up a position on a firing platform. They were low-ranking men and too old to go out on horseback but solid enough to defend the gate.

When the refugees returned to the garrison house, Harold pulled out his rifle and started to clean it. His mother gave him a wary look. "Why are you doing that?" she asked.

"Just in case I get called by the militia," replied Harold.

She pulled back and gave him a hard look before answering. "I hope it doesn't come to that."

Harold replied enthusiastically, "I got one of the men in the militia to let me know when the bulk of the Bavianer were killed. He said he'd call me to go out of the city and help out when things were safer. He'll send a message on the comms device!"

Gladys looked at the family comms device warily. No message had yet come in. She looked at her son. He was starting to look like his father. His shoulders were beginning to broaden. "I don't know about that," was all she said.

As soon as she said those words, Nellie and Naomi immediately started to beg their mother to go to the stores of Hattusa. Harold didn't want to go. He wanted to continue to clean his rifle and prepare for the call. "I'll join you later."

Outside, Francis joined in a game of stickball.

Harold carefully took apart his rifle. It had a lever action, and such a rifle was common in every household in Illissos. The militia carbines were a great deal more advanced. For one thing, they were smaller. They also had a special sight that helped with aiming during the constant twilight conditions. His rifle had a low-light sight, but it was by no means as advanced as the sights on the militia carbines.

In addition to the living quarters, which held the room where Harold's family slept during the sieges, the garrison house had a corral and livery stable for livestock brought in from the farms in the surrounding country. Harold's camels were out of sight in the stable. The corral held several domestic animals, including a large bull that quietly fed upon hay. Several sheepdogs were resting in the nearby kennel.

Harold did not feel like playing stickball with Francis or any of the other kids. He couldn't focus on anything except for the excitement of possibly going on the Bavianer hunt. Once his rifle was cleaned, he put it aside and went to kill time by pacing around the garrison house. The natural place to go was the largest room, the communal great room. During Bavianer swarms, all the refugees used the room, which was larger than Harold's entire house, as a cafeteria and meeting place. On the far side of the room was a buffet.

At present it didn't hold any food, and its stainless steel containers were clean and empty. Five circular tables were spread out in the center of the room. The tops of the tables were plastic but colored in a faux wood pattern. The room and tables were empty except for a gray-bearded man. Harold had seen the man hand the garrison house landlady some paperwork earlier. The man's beard hung to the nape of his neck, and a scar traveled from just below his left eye to the corner of his mouth. To the man's left was a gray, felted traveling cloak. In his right hand, he held a large clay pipe from which a rich, sweet tobacco smoke emerged in a blue, cloudy stream. In front of the man, a large map was spread out. Harold thought for a second that this bearded man was a songwriting "folkie," but a look into his eyes showed a serious man. Such a serious man didn't write or sing traditional songs. Nor did he perform them for children at fairs. "Have the men of the militia gone outside?" he asked.

"Yes, sir," replied Harold.

"Good. The sooner they do their job, the sooner life can return to normal," replied the gray-bearded man.

"Indeed, sir," replied Harold. He then asked, "Is that a local map, sir? Is it a map of Hattusa?"

The gray-bearded man replied, "Yes. I've been compelled to look at it all day." He took a puff from his pipe.

"Why have you been compelled to look at the map all day?" asked Harold.

"I just have a feeling," answered the bearded man mysteriously.

Harold looked at the map. It was a detailed topographical map, which showed navigational lines running along the four cardinal directions. Elevation and contour lines were prominent, and all terrain features were represented in detail.

The map was centered on the Mighty River, the great stream New Lydia, Santa Fe, and Hattusa were built next to. If one looked to the left of the map, the city of New Lydia straddled the river where it flowed into a great lake. New Lydia was the most advanced, wealthy and populous of the three cities. From the New Lydian mouth of the Mighty River, the river took a great bend around a mountain range. At the bend was Santa Fe. Further upstream was Hattusa. Upstream from Hattusa was the great basin, so called because the mountain ranges to either side of the river made the appearance of a basin on a map. The source of the Mighty River was a great glacier field in the northern mountains.

The man turned to Harold and said, "My name is Greamand." He then pointed to the map. "If you go downhill from here and continue to go east"—Greamand pointed to a downward slope on the east side of Hattusa—"you can get to Aviabron." He then pointed off the map onto the table— the rough location of Aviabron. It seemed to Harold to be a long way.

Greamand continued, "If you cut across the mountains here"—at this, he pointed to a range of mountains—"you can cut the distance to New Lydia. So far, there are only shepherd trails through, but perhaps one day, there will be a major road."

Harold's eyes looked at a dotted line between Santa Fe and Hattusa. Words were written next to it—"Railway line proposed." No railway line connected the cities as yet, but Harold had heard rumors that such a track would be built. Harold then looked carefully at the area on the map representing the rolling terrain around Hattusa, and he pointed to it. "This area is what I need to worry about." He then told his plan to Greamand about joining the militia when the tide of battle turned.

Greamand looked at him carefully, "Do you have the comms device now?"

Harold suddenly realized that his mother had the comms device, and she was off shopping. Sergeant Burbeen could have signaled right now, and he'd miss his chance. Harold mumbled something polite, his face turned red, and he left the great room and the gray-bearded man at a run.

Harold arrived in the city center. The buildings there were packed together and made of the mud-straw mixture that was the common building material used on Illissos. The city center was constructed to take up a minimum of space; therefore, the walls didn't' need to be so large. And the city center was designed for pedestrians. Today the narrow streets held many pedestrians. The many refugees were using the dull minutes that ticked away slowly during a siege for shopping. Some said the merchants of Hattusa prayed to the gods of the Ancient Faith for a Bavianer swarm.

The narrow streets were a colorful, moving river of Illissos settlers in fine felt or twill clothes milling about, browsing, buying, and selling.

Harold passed one worried-looking woman who was looking at her comms device. "Nothing!" she muttered.

Suddenly Harold turned a corner and ran into Julie, a girl from school with whom he'd had an on-again off-again crush. Julie and her family also stayed in the garrison houses during the sieges. "There's going to be a dance at the garrison house," she said. "Perhaps you could come?"

Harold couldn't believe it; she wanted to dance with him. With surprising clarity, Harold calculated what he should do. If he was held up in the city, he might as well go to a dance, but should the call come in, he would leave to fight the Bavianer. He imagined Julie, with tears in her eyes, insisting she would wait for his return as he got the call and left to fight. He promised Julie he'd be at the dance.

"Great!" replied Julie, and she turned on her heels and disappeared into the crowd, leaving Harold alone.

But he was alone only for a minute. Harold walked twenty more steps and ran into his mother and sisters looking over turquoise necklaces. As they looked, an excited, fat man ran by and exclaimed that gunfire had been heard and it was very likely that the militia had destroyed the main part of the Bavianer force. "They've laid waste to them!" the fat man shouted. "They'll come back real soon now!"

The news ripped through the milling shoppers. Harold could see the sighs of relief from the women whose husbands, brothers, and sons were on active service. A militiaman walked through the crowd wearing his uniform. Harold watched with jealousy as the women and girls eyed him. He was glad to see that Julie wasn't around; had she looked at the militiaman like that, his heart would have sunk like a stone. Harold also noticed his mom and sisters looked at the soldier with starry eyes.

"Mom," asked Harold, "is there any message for me on the comms device?"

She took out the handheld flat screen. "No," she replied.

"Let me see." Harold grabbed the device in a hurried way and looked—no messages.

Harold then typed out a message to Sergeant Burbeen and instantly got a response, though not from Burbeen. It was from the comms center at Hattusa. It read:

> TO KEEP THE MILITIA FREE OF DISTRACTIONS AND SHARPLY LOOKING FOR BAVIANER, ALL MILITIA COMMS DEVICE ACCOUNTS

HAVE BEEN DEACTIVATED FOR THE
DURATION OF THE EMERGENCY.
WHEN THE SIEGE IS LIFTED, YOU
MESSAGE WILL BE DELIVERED.

WE APOLOGIZE FOR THE
INCONVENIENCE.

Harold was taken aback by the message. If messages out to the militia were blocked, what about militia messages from the militia back to the city? Had he been double-crossed by Sergeant Burbeen? Had Burbeen know the comms devices would be shut down and deliberately made a promise he couldn't keep? Harold thought very hard about this. He hadn't seen any hint of treachery in the sergeant's face. Harold didn't know what to make of the situation. He decided to return to the garrison house and wait out the situation. At any moment, the comms accounts could be reactivated and he could get a message.

He walked home in confusion. Along the way, he noticed several priests putting more incense in the sacred fire. They were saying prayers, but he couldn't hear the words.

The Low-Fullday supper at the garrison house was filled with chatting, happy refugees, impatiently awaiting the return of the militia. The story about the gunfire had made the local radio station's news broadcast, and bets were made in the Hattusa market whether the troopers would return during Decent or Fulldark.

As usual during the sieges, the garrison house food consisted of dried and canned items. The bread, however, was freshly baked by some of the women in the house and Harold was enjoying its sweet taste greatly when he looked over at the gray-bearded man. He wasn't eating. Instead, he continued to look over his map and other papers on the table. Harold wanted to go see what insight the old man had possibly discovered, but the excitement of the siege had run its course, and the crash had come. He could barely keep his eyes open. He dragged himself to bed and fell fast asleep. That Descent, he dreamed of text messages in the clouds. The white puffs arranged themselves into a word that said:

TROUBLE

***

"The gates are still closed," said Francis at first Fulldark. Harold and Francis had walked to the city walls while they killed time awaiting breakfast. "The militia isn't saying all that much about when they think the riders will return."

"They should come in soon if so many shots were heard," replied Harold as the two boys watched militiamen guarding the walls. When watching the soldiers got old, they returned to the garrison house. "I wonder why the militia guards at the gates are so glum?" asked Harold as they walked into the garrison house's great room.

"I guess that they don't want to start any rumors," said Francis.

"It isn't like there aren't any rumors already," said Harold.

Suddenly, a warm, deep voice intruded on the two boys' conversation. "This is called the fog of war." It was Greamand. Despite having spoken with Greamand before, Harold was surprised by the interruption. Harold was still at the phase of life where he did not expect to be conversed with by adults as if he was on equal terms with them. Harold's conversations with his mother were still one-way affairs, with much nagging and scolding. After Harold's father's death two years ago, he very rarely left the farm, except to attend school. To be addressed as an equal, to have a conversation worthy of interruption by an adult was, indeed, strange.

As he surveyed Greamand, Harold was struck by the mystery of the man. He had a priestly name, but Greamand was clearly not wearing the normal clothes of a priest. Instead of the bright red cloak, this man wore a russet frock, and his hat was a large, broad brimmed felt hat that was a shade of gray three times darker than the man's beard.

"What have *you* heard?" Francis asked Greamand.

"Nothing but rumors," answered Greamand. "I do have an unsettled feeling about this siege, though. Have you noticed that the mayor's office isn't releasing any news? Additionally, the sacred fire has had several additional offerings of incense."

Harold had noticed additional offerings, but didn't know what to make of them. He looked at Greamand without smiling. What about Sergeant Burbeen? What was going to happen?

"But the gunfire!" said Francis. "Surely this will be over soon. Bavianer can't operate guns."

"Yes, of course," said Greamand. He then lit his pipe and began to smoke but said no more.

***

While the garrison house refugees ate the Fulldark breakfast, Harold's mother expressed her worry about the missing militia. She drew her lips tight so that her mouth made a single dark line. Rumors swirled that the militia had come upon some sort of a calamity. After Fullday ended, the deepening blue twilight gave the Bavianer an advantage over the militia and their horses. A shepherd from the outer Santa Fe District, temporarily trapped by the siege and wearing a woolen, hooded jacket woven in a tweed pattern, named Murdo MacRae insisted that hope wasn't lost. "Even during Fulldark, a group of men can hold off Bavianer if they circle up right. I've taken my sheep all over this area and make sure I spend the twilight and dark times on the hilltops, away from where the beasts catch bonefish and where they don't like to stay. I hope the militia is out there doing just that and that they are racking up a high body count."

Harold hoped that some Bavianer would still be around when he was old enough to join the militia. High body counts weren't what he wanted.

***

While the worried refugees awaited the return of the militia, the dance Julie had mentioned to Harold was finally at hand. Julie was wearing a felt dress of emerald green. Harold could barely breathe when she came into the dance hall. At the same time, Harold was divided between the dueling desires to dance with Julie and to await a militia call. After carefully balancing the twin desires in his mind, Harold figured that he could dance while he waited for the call from the militia. The garrison house refugees tuned the radio to the traditional music station at the time the radio schedule promised square dancing music. In the great room, the refugees cleared away the tables and chairs in the great hall and paired off. Harold partnered with his sister, with Julie as his "neighbor," while his mother partnered with Murdo MacRae.

The music played; the dancers went around in a square and changed partners so that Harold was dancing with Julie. All through the dance, Julie went through the motions but didn't bother to look at him. She wasn't even very friendly. While Harold and Julie danced, Harold's mother was now dancing in the lead with a woman whose husband was out with the militia, while Murdo had taken his other sister as a partner. There were more women than men on account of the militia being gone.

Suddenly, a tremendous noise like ripping linen drowned out the music. Seconds later, a series of terribly loud bangs filled the air. Then the radio made a horrid squeaking sound and cut off entirely. Harold's sisters grabbed their ears and screamed. A look of fright went over the faces of the women, including Harold's mother. The shock wave from the booms pinched Harold's eardrums so that he felt two great stabs of pain in his ears while the air itself turned hard.

Then, as suddenly as the deafening interruption had happened, it was over. There was silence, and the air resumed its normal pressure. During the attack, Harold had not felt fear, or really any emotion whatsoever. But after the last explosion, his hands shook uncontrollably. Julie ran from the room in tears, and the older women shifted from screams of fear to sudden talking. The women didn't converse so much as talk out loud about their feelings to everyone at once but nobody in particular. A portly woman shouted at the top of her lungs, "What was that?! What was that?! What *was* that!"

The radio was now out. All Hattusa stations were silent. Those with handheld comms devices looked at them with fear—silence!

Greamand stood up. "I fear this siege is more than a normal Bavianer attack."

Chapter 3

A CAMPAIGN AGAINST US

Greamand's words hit the refugees at the Garrison House with a collective fist to the stomach. He continued. "These explosions aren't an accident. They are part of the campaign against us."

"Whatever do you mean *campaign*?" asked a woman holding a squirming toddler.

"I think someone is out to destroy our city, to alter our hold on this part of the moon. The Bavianer swarm was nothing more than a prop to draw out the militia." Harold expected that Greamand would say more, but he didn't. Instead, he continued in a forceful voice, "Who is in charge of this garrison house?"

Harold looked around. After what seemed a long delay, the portly landlady raised her hand. "I own the house. I get paid a nominal fee from the city government to keep it ready for these emergencies. As you all can see, I keep a good house! What are you trying to say?"

"You do indeed keep a good house, madam," replied Greamand. "Since you are recognized by the city to care for all of us"—Greamand gestured to the assembled refugees—"I propose you form a delegation to go to the city government and see what is happening and offer our services in support."

"I don't want to do that!" exclaimed the portly housemother. "I'm already helping out with this house."

"Indeed you are, madam," said Greamand in a reassuring way. "I propose you appoint someone to act on your, and all of our, behalf."

"I appoint you then, seeing as you seem to have all the answers," she curtly replied.

"These two boys"—Greamand pointed to Harold and Francis—"will also come with me. And you, good shepherd"—he pointed to the Santa Fe shepherd Murdo MacRae—"I'll need your expertise."

All the time Greamand was speaking, Harold could feel that he would get called to help, but instead of the excitement he'd felt from his vain effort to join the militia, he felt a worrisome electric sensation that went straight down to his toes. He caught his breath, and he could feel a heat that came from some frightened place in his mind rest upon his face. Afterward, Harold would remember the sensation as a mixture of dread and anticipation. Somehow, he knew that a visit to the government house would lead on to a dangerous journey. He looked over at his mother. He half expected that she would insist that he stay. But she only looked at him with a fearful longing. She didn't say anything; instead, she only nodded.

Greamand, Murdo the shepherd, Harold, and Francis formed up in the garrison house great room to leave as a group, but before they left, Harold turned and gave his mother and sisters each a hug. His mother gripped him with a sort of frenzy but didn't stop him from leaving. Her reaction gave Harold chills.

31

As the group took their first steps away from the garrison house, Francis turned to Greamand and asked, "Why did you make such a point to get appointed to go see the city government?"

"Because," answered Greamand, "of human group dynamics. There is no hard and fast rule to this, and I often go by gut instinct in these cases. Normally, with a group, the person who controls the resource that the group is dependent upon is the leader, if not officially by letter than by unwritten fact. In this case, the refugees of the garrison house were looking to the landlady for leadership. I figured that she didn't want to do more than provide room and board, so I stepped up. However, I needed to get some legitimacy to do so. If you get legitimacy to act in others' names, you gain a great deal in support from others and less resentment than otherwise."

"What other support do you think we'll get from the garrison house?" asked Harold. He then continued, "Why didn't you just go and see the mayor as a regular citizen?"

"There is always resentment when a person takes charge of anything. In this case, I wanted help from the garrison house to get assistants. Namely"—at this, Greamand gestured to his three companions—"help from you three. I needed permission from the mothers of you two youngsters." The way Greamand said *permission* sounded funny to Harold—that is to say funny in an ominous way, like when one is tricked into doing something difficult. Greamand continued, "I know the mayor. He'll see me no matter what."

The garrison house was a property containing the large house as well as a corral and barn. It was also situated near one of the city walls, so the easiest way for the group to make it to the city hall was to walk along the road that was between some town house buildings and the outer wall. As they neared one of the smaller auxiliary gates that lead to the Mighty River, they came upon a small crowd. Greamand walked through it, the others behind him in a single line.

"Whew!" whistled Murdo.

The crowd surrounded a dead man in a respectful semicircle. Harold had never seen a man who looked quite like this one. His chest had several bullet holes, and blood was leaking from them and pooling on the gaps between the cobblestones. It was his face that struck Harold as so strange. In basic appearance, it reminded him of his loyal camel Clem's face, but unlike Clem's normal gentle expression, this man had died in a rage. A coat of intense anger was painted upon it. His lips were curled back, locked in an expression of pure hatred. He had dark, curly hair. Harold looked at the man for what seemed like an eternity. Simultaneously, he felt a sense of pity for the dead man and relief that such a hate-filled stranger was gone. A sergeant with a limp started to shoo the gawkers away.

Greamand looked at the militia sergeant and asked, "What happened here?"

"The deceased, sir, tried to open the gate. He was shot dead," said the militia sergeant.

"Do you know who he was?" asked Greamand.

"No, sir," replied the militia sergeant. "He had garrison house papers, though. He wasn't from this city. He nearly had the gate wide open before we shot. If he'd gotten the gate open, it would have been the end for all of us. There are Bavianer just outside the door. The Bavianer could have rushed into the city."

With that ominous statement, the group moved on. In the twilight gloom, Harold couldn't help but wonder if more treacherous people were in the city, trying to open the gates from the inside.

Harold had never seen the inside of the government house. In the past, Harold had spent the siege days bottled up in Hattusa caring for his livestock at the garrison house, playing stickball, and going to the shopping district and square. He realized now that he'd been wasting time with childish things. He could have used the time meeting with notables and seeing how the city's political process worked.

The hall was just off the square. The foursome arrived at the town square and took a road past Pioneer Park to the hall. The doors were open, and Greamand led the group into the main lobby. He approached the visitors' desk and announced that he wished to see the mayor.

"He won't see anyone right now," said the short-haired secretary.

"Take a message to him," replied Greamand. "I am appointed, with these assistants, representative of Garrison House Southeast Four to speak to him on matters of concern."

"There are many garrison houses," replied the secretary curtly. "You can wait, but he might not see you immediately."

Harold could feel a rising anger at the secretary's brisk response, but before he could say anything, Greamand smiled, put a single finger gently on the secretary's desk, and spoke in a voice that was both charming and forceful enough that it was hard to ignore. "My name is Greamand. I know the mayor. Tell him that I'm here. He'll be happy that you let him know I'm here and will adjust his schedule to see us."

He said the words forcefully but with respect. Harold couldn't help noticing that there was a gravitas, a timbre to his voice that conveyed wisdom. Harold's temper instantly evaporated into calm.

The secretary looked up at Greamand, and then she looked at the others. Harold could see her calculate the risks of telling the mayor about the visitors versus leaving potentially important people in the waiting room for an indefinite amount of time. At least Greamand might be important. Harold had the feeling that, if he'd approached the mayor's office on his own, he would not have gotten an audience at all.

After an awkward pause, the secretary slowly got up from her seat and went back through a door, to where, presumably, the mayor's private office was.

While they waited for the secretary to allow them audience with the mayor or give them a curt dismissal, Harold looked around. The interior of the government house was well lit, with floating, cordless electric lights; they were the type of lights that could be easily shipped and hung anywhere. Harold reckoned they'd been transported from Earth through the spaceport and were worth ten times in Hattusa what they'd be in a living room not on the far frontier. Harold then looked around at the mural showing the early pioneers from New Lydia headed along the Mighty River in steamboats and covered wagons. It had only been fort-five Boreas years since the settlers had come to found this city, in its key spot on the river and mountains. Many of the children shown in the mural were still alive, though with gray hair and grandchildren by now. Until this threatening situation, Harold had never realized how important his community was to him. Harold watched a robot dust the furniture. Its body made a mechanical whirring noise. Another robot was buffing the floor.

A shout interrupted his thoughts. "Greamand!" The mayor was walking toward the gray-bearded man with his hand out.

"Mayor Winchurst," replied Greamand, who took his hand and shook it.

Introductions were made and the mayor led the group into a back room with great insistence.

The group walked past the secretary toward the mayor's office. While they walked, Harold overheard the mayor say in a low voice to Greamand, "I heard about your banishment from New Lydia. I wish you to know that I supported you, although I have no voice there."

Greamand answered in an equally low voice, "Thank you, though I think that the banishment did me good. Nobody should be bitter at those who push you toward the light."

The mayor continued, "I can't begin to express my gratitude for all the great advice and mentorship you gave to me while I was growing up in New Lydia. I resented it as a teen, but once I turned twenty-five, everything you did for me came into clear focus. You always have a voice here."

"Thanks," replied Greamand. Then in a louder voice, Greamand pointed to his three companions and said, "These three are with me. Whatever happens next, I want them to be part of it." He then paused. "Mayor Winchurst, we will need help, and this situation is very dangerous."

The mayor looked back at Greamand. "How right you are," he answered with a sigh.

What Harold had presumed would be a back room private office turned out to be a well-lit conference room. A large map of the city was prominently featured on the wall. Harold noticed arrows, circles, and other symbols on the map. A militia captain with a metal prosthetic leg was in the room. "Greamand," said the mayor, "allow me to introduce Captain Fleck. He is in command of the defense of this city."

As introductions were made, the captain looked at the mayor with questioning eyes.

The mayor gave a nod. "It's all right to brief them. We'll need all the help we can get now."

Captain Fleck moved to a map on the wall, and as he did so, his metal leg made a light clang. "Please take your seats, gentlemen, and I will brief you on the situation."

Captain Fleck was wearing the woolen militia uniform colored Illissos beige. On his good foot, the foot of flesh and blood, was a black leather boot. It was polished but not to a parade ground-worthy high sheen. His metal leg started just below the knee. It was a very crude prosthetic. Harold wondered why the captain didn't have the advanced artificial limbs he'd heard about at school. Why were floating lights, but not the latest in medical technology, imported from Earth?

Before Harold could ponder the unfairness of life and question the mayor about priorities, Captain Fleck's briefing was interrupted by a forceful jab of words from the mayor. "None of what he tells you can leave this room!" He then added softly, "I'll make the announcement to the city myself."

Captain Fleck continued, "Our militia met with disaster when they sallied outside to strike the Bavianer."

At this, Harold flinched. The dream, the one where the clouds had become a message—Trouble"—had it been a sign? Harold puzzled over the dream and offered up a silent prayer, but no answer seemed to come.

Captain Fleck continued, "As far as the command post here has been able to discern via the battlefield update reports sent by our militia, the troop of riders met with a small party of Bavianer and proceeded to attack them. They killed most of the beasts, but several escaped up this draw here." He pointed to a part of the map where there was a large, hand-drawn arrow. Harold looked at the arrow; it was red, and an X had been drawn midway through the arrow.

"What does that X mean?" he asked.

Captain Fleck responded. "I'll get to that." He continued, "The riders pursued, presuming that they were headed toward the main group of the attacking Bavianer. At this point, what happened is not fully clear. But it seems the horsemen met with a group of humans allied with the Bavianer. These humans were armed with machine guns and had sowed the upper part of the draw with mines specially designed to kill horses and their riders. The commander of the force was killed outright." Here the captain pointed to the X. "Then another officer took charge and ordered the men to make a fighting retreat down the draw. It seems here that an enemy force had blocked the draw and continued to mow down the ranks of our militia. The remainders of the militia took to the high ground here." Captain Fleck pointed to a circle. "And they held out until destroyed by a mixed human and Bavianer force. The gunshots heard by the city likely came from this encounter. The sounds of the firing could possibly carry to the city from this location, but gunfire would likely be acoustically masked in the draw where the first encounter took place."

Murdo sighed. "You mean they're all gone?"

"Yes," said Captain Fleck dryly.

Francis made a small cry and then stifled it. Harold looked over at Francis; his face crumpled, and then he recovered and gave the captain a sorrowful look.

Captain Fleck looked back at Francis. "Your father?"

Francis only nodded.

"I'll make the announcement when I make the statement to the city about the artillery fire," said Mayor Winchurst.

Harold wondered how the city would take such an announcement. This was an epic disaster. All the fine clothes the mayor had, his mansion, his salary, no doubt lavish, were suddenly small compensation for the task of telling a hundred women that they were widows.

"You mean the explosions that destroyed the comms center were fired from a cannon battery?" asked Murdo.

"They are precision-guided munitions rockets. I've seen the shattered pieces of the rockets personally. Each rocket struck the communications center in a perfect way. Our city is cut off by means of electronic communications from the rest of Illissos," said Captain Fleck.

"Who would do such a thing?" asked Greamand

"Ari Laybeter," said the Mayor Winchurst.

"Who?" asked Harold.

"A good question," said the mayor. "Greamand, do you know this man? Have you heard of this person in your many travels?"

Greamand was silent. He looked down and shook his head no. "How do you know it was this Ari Laybeter?" asked Greamand.

"He announced himself to one of the gate guards from outside the wall," answered the mayor. "I spoke to him this Descent. He has asked us to surrender."

A knock at the conference-room door interrupted the discussion. The mayor opened it, and in walked Hattusa's high priestess. She was a large woman with a round, rosy face and short hair that was a dirty blonde. She walked hunched forward. Harold noticed that her walk was a crude, deliberate imitation of a man's walk, somewhat like the toughest miner on the mountain. Harold looked at the high priestess carefully. Her fingernails were long, and her hands had nothing like calluses from work. The way she walked struck Harold as an act. It seemed a ploy to intimidate people. Watching her walk, Harold realized that Bogedet the high priestess had gained her office through sheer loud bullying. Harold figured that she was able to bully others from a position of invulnerability; any hostile response to her actions would be automatically deflected by the fact she was a woman, and a heavier, less-than-attractive one at that.

Before he could continue with his thoughts, Bogedet brayed out, "Mr. Mayor, we should take up the offer and surrender. We should ask for their terms."

Mayor Winchurst answered. "I've already discussed this with you. I am not going to surrender the city until I know that we cannot get help from New Lydia."

The high priestess's eyes went from Mayor Winchurst to Harold, Francis, and Murdo and then locked on Greamand. Her eyes filled with a hot hatred, and an angry sneer came upon her face. "What," the High Priestess intoned slowly "is *he* doing here?" Her face became purple with rage, and her body quivered.

Harold looked at Greamand. He said nothing; his face was neutral and calm, and he looked back at the high priestess of Hattusa without flinching.

"He is a guest of this administration," replied the mayor. "He is an official garrison house representative to …"

She cut him off. "Do you know who he *is*? What he's *done*!" she spat out the words.

"Madam High Priestess!" the mayor answered back sharply. "I have a duty as mayor to discuss civic matters with the citizens and residents of this city. And in this case, I am meeting with garrison house representatives." The mayor stood up. "The two of us have business to talk about related to this siege, but we cannot discuss it together in front of these representatives." Here the mayor made a subtle gesture toward the boys.

The high priestess looked over the two boys and then Murdo. Her lips turned down to a frown, and the red color drained away from her face.

"I suggest we speak later," said Mayor Winchurst. "I know this situation will bring passion, but it is best to converse privately."

Then the high priestess's face became red again, and she looked hard at Greamand, who remained silent. "I'll be back in thirty minutes." With that, she turned on her heels and walked out of the room. Her first few steps were normal, but then she took on the large, heavy strides Harold had noticed before.

"Thank you," said Greamand to the mayor. "That could have gotten very ugly. You have a way of managing people."

"I learned much of it from you, sir," said the mayor. "You, of course, know what must be done. The comms center is out. I have to send messengers."

"I take it you want us to serve as the messengers," said Greamand. "I believe you are more right than you may know about surrender. I think should this city open its gates, the Bavianer will kill everyone within, no matter what their human masters say. These humans, this Ari Laybeter, might not even be able to control the Bavianer that much. If we surrender to him, we also surrender to the Bavianer; with them in the city, we will be at their mercy. I don't think they will show us mercy."

"Right!" said Murdo. "Who knows what sort of rampage they'll go on?"

Greamand continued, "A regular Bavianer siege is a normal thing; it has something to do with their mating and migration behaviors. This siege with humans involved gives

41

it a darker hue." Greamand paused, took in a breath, and then said, "These men are filibusters."

"What is a filibuster?" asked Murdo.

"They are unofficial agents of a foreign power that act on their own to expand that foreign power's domination. Should they fail, the foreign power loses nothing; should they succeed, the foreign power will gain much. I suspect they wish to depopulate Hattusa and dam this valley."

"That means that the whole area would become a lake," said Murdo.

"Indeed," replied Greamand. "And if one is going to dam this river, why not divert the water toward Aviabron. All through last Fullday, I looked over the maps and went to the high towers and looked out. This place can be dammed up like some of those rivers in the American West on Earth. To build such a dam, the filibusters need this city to fall. To get us to fall, they must keep us bottled up until we surrender. Now is the last minute for them to take over. Soon, Hattusa will get rail service from Santa Fe, and our position here will be permanent. They have only a small window of time when they can take this area over. They must get us to surrender quickly.

"They can't have many more rockets, mines, or explosives," he reasoned. "There are no good roads between Hattusa and Aviabron, and they'd have had to pack in their supplies by mule, camel, or oxcart. They don't have Zeppelins, or they would have been noticed and used already. Plus antigravity systems are pretty hard to maintain." Greamand looked at one of the floating lights; it wobbled unsteadily—a telltale sign the antigravity devices were failing. "Aviabron might not have the facilities to fix them. New Lydia is barely able to keep the Zeppelins flying as it is. Other than the Bavianer, this must be a small operation on the part of the humans and their weaponry. And they're likely saving what they have left for a counterattack."

Greamand stopped, wrinkled his brow, and continued. "They may have made mistakes. They are inexperienced in a siege. They must be operating on a shoestring budget, but it doesn't matter. This situation is very dangerous. We've lost most of our fighting men. We must get to New Lydia and get help. New Lydia has a militia that can help us and a robust, competent government. Santa Fe"—Greamand made a sigh—"won't be able to help. We need to get the word out about this situation, especially to New Lydia. If the river is diverted, New Lydia will become a desert, and Santa Fe will dry up. Our entire culture will be destroyed. Our people will spend eternity begging for scraps from Aviabron."

Chapter 4

MESSENGER PLATOON SIX

The mayor stood up. "Captain Fleck, enlist these men in the militia; make them a special unit. Call 'em Messenger Platoon Six. They'll be numbered "six," and the next bunch of messengers will be "seven." That will keep our enemies guessing as to how many others we've sent out. Greamand, you will be the platoon sergeant. All others will be privates. Your enlistment will be for the duration of time it takes to deliver the message. You are to determine how to get this group out of the city and to New Lydia. I agree with you, Greamand, help from Santa Fe will be paltry, if it materializes at all. I will write a message that you will deliver to the government of New Lydia. Greamand, I will personally write two dispatches that you are to deliver to New Lydia; one must be given to Chairman Somerset of the Secular Authority, and the other must be read—by you—to the general public should the Secular Authority not accept the first dispatch."

"Aren't we a bit small to be a platoon?" asked Greamand.

"That's part of the same ruse in calling your team Messenger Platoon Six," answered Mayor Winchurst. "If they catch three or four people and you say you're part of a platoon, your captors will figure there are thirty more people somewhere nearby, and that could give you an edge."

At this, he dismissed Captain Fleck and the newly organized Messenger Platoon Six to plan its escape. Captain Fleck gestured to the four with a flip of his hand. Immediately, they all followed him through a doorway to a dingy, dark hall and then into a large room that was a military operations center. Harold noticed right away that there were no fashionable floating antigravity lights. Instead, the room was lit with regular light bulbs. Many of the tabletops were of rough, unpainted plywood. A single antigravity light shone on a large map of Hattusa. However, this antigravity light did not float, and having ceased floating, it was placed on a side so that the beam of light hit the map squarely in the center.

The map had been marked by arrows and other symbols like the map in the mayor's chambers, but the markings were made by a grease pencil. In the area outside the city's walls, especially near the gates, were circles, and within the circles were phrases such as "x12 Bav" and "x1 MG." Harold figured that the circles were the positions of the besiegers and their approximate number. MG, Harold reasoned, must stand for machine gun. He'd heard about those deadly weapons, but up until now, he'd never seen one. Because the main military action on Illissos involved human militia against primitive Bavianer, and the most effective way for the humans to fight Bavianer was mounted on horse or camel with a sword, the Illissos settlers had gone backward in military technology from the more competitive Earth militaries.

The group settled in and took seats in the room. Harold looked around. The militiamen all held higher ranks and, for the most part, were older and heavier than the lean, young crew that had left during the earlier Fullday. Lines of worry creased the militiamen's faces, and none smiled. A radio and communications setup sat in one corner, but it didn't appear to work. A flashing, angry red light was the only indicator of functionality, and its only function was to warn the user that communications was down.

Francis looked exhausted. Harold halfway thought that Francis would become sick or faint. After they sat down, there was an awkward pause. Murdo looked down at his shoes. Then Captain Fleck spoke. "First I have to figure out how to get you out of the city and able to travel overland to New Lydia, or at least Santa Fe. Other than one pack mule, I don't have many more animals to spare. The cavalry horses are now either captured by the enemy outside or have been eaten by the Bavianer."

"I have three camels. I can take them out of the livery stable at the garrison house," said Harold. As soon as he said it, Harold realized that his voice conveyed too much eagerness.

Captain Fleck looked at him, his face blank, and replied, "There are four of you."

"Francis and I can ride double," said Harold.

"That will make this harder. There are Bavianer all outside of this city. Another person would just be more of a burden for a camel," said Greamand.

"You mean I can't go?" asked Francis.

"Was your father with the militia?" asked Greamand.

"Yes," replied Francis; his face fell even further.

Harold looked at Francis. It appeared that Francis was going to be cut from the team before they even got outside the city.

"You are a bit young, and we should be frank here. Your mother is now a widow. Do you think she should also lose you?" interrupted Captain Fleck.

Francis shrunk a bit further, breathed in, and recovered his composure.

Harold decided that now was not the time to mention that his father had been killed by Bavianer too.

"But that's a moot point," continued Captain Fleck. "I have to get you three"—he pointed to Greamand, Murdo, and Harold here—"the mule, and your camels out of the city and away from the besieged area so that you all can make a break for New Lydia or at least get to a government office at Santa Fe where a message can be sent."

"We can possibly send a message from Santa Fe," said Greamand, "but this dispatch must be delivered to New Lydia. We must be able to lobby for aid. New Lydia's leadership could become very slow in calling out their militia. I must be there to impart the seriousness of the situation, not just to Hattusa but to all of our people on the river valley. Additionally, I'm not so sure we can trust every government official on Illissos, even priests of our faith."

Murdo looked at Greamand. "Why do you say that?"

Greamand answered, "There are cracks developing in our religion, extreme differences of opinion. We Hattusa settlers are facing this crisis at a time when many of the clergy are quite angry at each other. Some might be willing to collaborate with our enemies to settle personal scores. We cannot expect to send a message from a comms center in Santa Fe and get a squadron of New Lydian horsemen to automatically ride out and save us. We really need to speak face-to-face with the Secular Authority in New Lydia. We'll need to make our journey with our eyes open to all threats."

"That will just make things harder," replied Murdo flatly.

"Who is the Secular Authority?" asked Harold.

"It is the elected government of New Lydia. It is the people who manage regular matters, such as street sweeping, law enforcement, and military operations," replied Greamand. He then continued, "I know Chairman Somerset; he's in charge there now."

"Just a second," asked Murdo. "Why don't we just get out of the city and to a high enough point so our comms devices can catch the signal from Santa Fe? From there, we just make the call to New Lydia. The mayor can record a message that can be forwarded on any of our comms devices."

"We've thought of that earlier," replied Captain Fleck. All comms devices have data tags, which indicate they are normally on the Hattusa network. We figure all comms devices with such a tag can be tracked. They are always sending out a signal that gives their location. If you don't travel with one, your chances of getting through increase; the besiegers are very likely economizing on human patrols and will attempt catch any messengers by only tracking comms devices. No phone, no tracking. You'll get through because they can't track a comms device you're not carrying."

"I wouldn't trust the Santa Fe network anyway," said Greamand.

"I have an idea about how we can get out of the walls unseen," said Harold.

Everyone looked at him.

Harold continued. He was a farm kid and had lived outside the walls his entire life. He felt like he had something valuable to say, and he knew it was time to contribute. "The Bavianer love salt licks. I've seen them fight over them before. Not six months ago, there were several of the creatures at my farmstead. They were between me and the house. I was afraid they'd eat me or one of the cows, but instead, they were fighting over a salt block I'd left out the

Orbweek earlier. I had a red lens flashlight and shone it in their eyes. They were dazzled, and I was able to slip by them toward the house. When I turned the light off, they went back to fighting over the salt."

"The red light must boggle them," speculated Murdo. "This was during Ascent, Descent, or Fulldark? When the sky and everything is twilight blue?"

"Yes," replied Harold, "it was Descent, nearly Fulldark. I was doing the chores after waking up."

"I suspect the eyes of the Bavianer are adapted to see best in the blue light; the frequency of the red light must hurt them. I've heard something like this before," added Greamand. "Where did you get the red lens flashlight?"

"It was one of the standard militia flashlights; the lens came with the light. I only used the red lens as a novelty. I wanted to see what it was like. I purchased it in Hattusa when I was thirteen," replied Harold.

Harold pointed to the map. "Here, at that small gate, we could get through on the camels. If I'm reading the symbols on that map right, there are only three Bavianer next to it. It could be that the gate is not watched or not watched by any humans. We could get through that and be gone."

"I know they really like salt too," said Murdo. "Our enemies probably don't see that small gate as important. This could work."

"Men, we haven't a moment to lose," said Captain Fleck. His eyes shone like a man who saw what to do and how to do it. "We've been watching that very gate for some time now and think it is possible to escape from it," he continued. "Francis, you will go to the front gate and attempt—no you will *make*—a distraction with the salt and red light. I'll have the other militiamen alongside you shoot down Bavianer while they fight for the salt. This will distract the

49

humans also, as it will definitely signal our intent to not surrender. This could also trick them in to thinking we are going to make an attack—a sally—out of the front gate. Greamand, Murdo, and Harold, you will take the camels from your garrison house and head for help, with your eventual destination New Lydia. While the Bavianer and humans are distracted, we might be able to get you through the small gate and on your way."

"Once we're out of the city, where do we go?" asked Murdo. Murdo's question was loud and clear, but nobody responded.

The militiamen manning the operations center stood up and looked at Captain Fleck. They were awaiting orders. Greamand was looking over at Francis and whispering something to him. It looked to Harold that he was either praying or giving him words of encouragement. The moment was so private that he looked away. They were speaking too softly to hear anyway.

Then Captain Fleck stretched out his arms to the four. "The trick is to get beyond the ring of besiegers, out to the Illissos scrubland beyond the river valley. You'll have complete freedom of movement once you're out of the ring. Get to New Lydia any way you want—over the mountains or to Santa Fe and take the train from there. You can even build a raft and float down the river. The point is, get away."

"I think it would be a good idea for the three of us to have a salt block and red lens flashlight also," said Murdo. "Francis and the others can drop the salt and shoot down from the city walls at the front gate, but we may need to create another distraction as we move out of the small gate."

"Francis," said Captain Fleck, "we have salt blocks in the cavalry stables and red lenses and militia rifles at the armory. You and the first sergeant will gather the supplies and return here."

Captain Fleck continued. "I will brief the mayor. Francis, once these three are supplied, the first sergeant will lead you to the front gate. He will lead the distraction effort. You will shine the red light and help out."

"Perhaps we should tell those at the garrison house what we are up to," said Greamand. "We'll tell in an indirect way of course; most of the garrison house will be asleep by now. Francis, you must also deliver a letter from me to the house's landlady. Perhaps, Harold, you should write a letter to your family if they aren't there to see us off."

"None of you say anything to anyone!" interrupted Captain Fleck, who had stopped in his tracks and turned around when Greamand started to talk about telling the plan to the refugees at the garrison house. "We need you to be a long way off before the mayor lets anyone know that he has sent messengers. We think"—he paused here—"we *know* there are spies in this city working with the besiegers. Get the camels and get to the small gate like we talked about. I'll meet you there with the pack mule. The mule can carry your food rations. No letters."

Harold shook hands with Francis. "Fool 'em good."

Francis looked Harold in the eyes. Francis had brown eyes; before this time, Harold had seen Francis as a kid, but Francis now held an adult's wisdom in his eyes. Harold figured that his eyes had made the same transformation. Harold couldn't help it, but his heart swelled with pride that he had been picked to go on this trip. He felt also a mild pity that Francis would need to stay behind.

***

Francis returned into the room with two blocks of salt and red lens flashlights for all. Immediately following him was the first sergeant. Francis distributed the flashlights and gave Murdo a brick of salt. The first sergeant gave Harold a heavy, woolen militia coat and gloves for the cold they were certain to face if they crossed the mountains. Murdo and Greamand had said they already had comfortable traveling clothes. They were all issued rifles and ammo. Harold was disappointed with the rifles; he'd have preferred the sleek, modern carbines. These were wooden stock rifles that fired eight shots from a clip, which was loaded from the top. They were heavy. The sights were iron sights—less advanced than those on his farm rifle.

After slinging the rifle across his back, Harold couldn't help but ask, "Will we get sabers too?"

"No," replied the first sergeant curtly, "unless you go to the battlefield outside and pick one up."

After being equipped, the trio made their way to the garrison house. The house was dark, the refugees within asleep, so Murdo and Greamand quietly grabbed their traveling clothes and rejoined Harold in the stable. He had three camels saddled with saddlebags, blankets and bedrolls included. Harold's militia rifle was loaded and ready to fire with a quick flick of the safety switch. They moved out and met Captain Fleck at the small gate, which led to the wooded park outside the city.

"Wait here until you hear firing from the main gate," instructed Captain Fleck. "When I give the signal, the guard will open the gate and out you go. I have spotters on the wall. We don't see any humans, and there is a man to provide covering fire if needed nonetheless. You'll have to lead your camels through the gate. It's too small for mounted riders." Captain Fleck handed Harold a leader rope so that he could also lead the pack mule. On the mule's back was the food for the expedition.

"When we get out," whispered Murdo, "I'll throw this brick of salt as far off as I can. Any Bavianer possibly around will smell it and run to it."

Harold looked at the gate and protective wall and shuddered. Just outside was danger. His hands became sweaty, and a feeling of dread stabbed at his heart. What would happen if the Bavianer didn't fall for the salt ruse and went for them? What else could go wrong?

It felt like they had to wait by the gate forever. Harold was so filled with excitement he was about ready to start climbing the city wall. The city wall, Captain Fleck, the camels, and the houses and cobblestones on the street were shrouded in blue light. Suddenly, a rifle shot pierced the silence, and then more bangs followed. By the front gate, a flare went into the air. It was a bright, burning, magnesium light that cut through the blue twilight like a flaming sword. The firing continued, and then a machine gun burst ripped through the air. Captain Fleck nodded, and the gate was open. The distraction was successful. Harold and the others passed through the gate. It was a bit like a tunnel, and before they passed the tunnel completely, a mysterious cry, like a howl of pain, cut through the blue gloom.

Once outside, Murdo hurled the salt as far as he could toward several cottonwood trees that had been planted after being so carefully transported across the vast distance of space to Illissos. They mounted the camels and started their journey. All had their rifles on their lap and their red lens flashlights in hand. "Don't shoot unless you must!" said Greamand in a low voice, "We must get away quietly."

Harold heard a scuffle near the cottonwoods. Bavianer were there fighting over the salt block! The plan was working.

Murdo shone his red light toward the noise. A few turns through the park, and they were headed uphill, away from the lowland and away from Hattusa. All the while, Harold imagined that a deadly machine gun crew was waiting in the bushes. He waited for a burst of fire to cut through him and the others. He waited for the camel's cry of pain and terror and then the roars of the Bavianer closing in for the kill.

They kept moving. When Messenger Platoon Six got about one hundred yards from the gate, a dazzling light suddenly appeared, lasting only the time it takes to blink, followed instantly by a loud bang. Harold whipped Clem to get him to run. However, the mule didn't seem to respond. Harold was gripping the mule's leader rope with his left hand while holding the rifle in his right. He was gripping the rope very hard, so when the mule stayed put while Clem bolted forward, Harold's hand burned from the friction

Harold dropped the rope and turned around. The mule was lying on the ground. It had been hit with an explosive device. Perhaps, though Harold, a rocket had been fired from the grove of cottonwood trees. The mule's body was torn to shreds.

"Keep moving!" shouted Greamand.

Just then, a Bavianer snapped at Murdo's camel, King Faisal. Murdo pointed his rifle at the creature and fired one shot before King Faisal bucked and took off to the left. Harold, riding Clem, followed. The three camels ran as fast as they could in a near panic until they reached the hill where they estimated they were free of the main ring of besiegers.

They slowed down. The danger seemed less, but they all looked over their shoulders as they continued on.

Murdo gave a frustrated shout and then said, "It's quite hard to hit anything from the back of a camel."

"Anyone hurt?" asked Greamand.

"We lost the pack mule and the food," replied Harold.

Chapter 5

WHAT HAPPENED AT HAROLD'S FARM

From the top of the hill, the three headed down. Harold took one last view of Hattusa before the crest of the hill blocked his line of sight. He looked down at his left hand and shone his small, clip-on light upon it. His hand had a red burn on it, but the skin hadn't been rubbed off. He'd let go of the rope before becoming too injured.

"Look sharp!" said Murdo. "Get the light off! We are out of the immediate danger area, but Bavianer can still make trouble." It was still early Fulldark; every bush and shrub looked ominous.

Murdo let out a sigh and then said. "It will be a long slog all the way to New Lydia. It's a long slog even to Santa Fe. We'll need food. We can't go back to the city. We need to press on, get food along the way."

"The question is where and how," said Greamand. "We could raid a farmhouse, or we can buy some food along the way. As representatives of the Hattusa government, we can also buy food on credit billed to the Hattusa Treasury."

"I think raiding a farmhouse would be stealing," replied Harold. "Why not swing by my farm? We have preserved food in the barn, as well as in the house. We could even stay in the house and rest if necessary. The farm is on the way anyway."

They all agreed that was better.

"How far off is the farmstead?" asked Greamand. He pulled out his map from a satchel and pointed to their present location.

Harold maneuvered Clem next to Greamand and looked at the map. He pointed to a series of black squares next to a thin, dotted blue line showing a creek bed that filled with water if it rained enough and said, "There, that is the farm."

A route was planned, and Messenger Platoon Six headed toward the farm, making a detour where they thought Bavianer could be lurking. Harold looked up at the stars and thought this could end up being an easy run—just a case of getting the camels to keep walking.

As the farmstead came into view, Harold felt a sense of unease. Lights were on—lights he was sure they'd turned off before heading for the garrison house. On Illissos farms, electricity was generated by a windmill, and it was stored in a battery. As a result, keeping the lights off when not in use was very important. There was nothing like returning home to discover the power was completely drained. It wasn't the outside lights that were a concern, for they always blazed away during Fulldark. The outside lights were on a lamppost, which had its own independent battery and small propeller to use the wind for electricity. Instead, it was the kitchen lights that bothered him.

Suddenly, Harold saw someone. A man walked from the house. A light glowed in front of his face; he was smoking. The man had the lean look of a soldier. Harold froze and stopped Clem. Murdo and Greamand moved their camels to Harold's left and right.

"Who do you think they are?" asked Murdo.

"I think they're soldiers from Aviabron," replied Harold.

"Is there another farm?" asked Greamand.

"Why don't we just shoot them?" asked Murdo.

"Too risky," answered Greamand. "Who knows how many men are in the farmhouse? It only takes one of them to hide in a room and call for backup."

Greamand dismounted, and the others did likewise. They quietly moved to a brushy location where they could look at the farmhouse and barn without being seen.

"We can move to a different farmstead, farther away," said Murdo.

Greamand pulled out the map. The three looked at it carefully. Harold's farmhouse was just next to the great Illissos scrubland. From the house, the travelers could head to the mountains without encountering any other people. The other farmhouses were north with the largest collection being across the Mighty River. This farm belt was where most of the refugees in Hattusa originated.

Harold spoke next, "We can't cross the river easily. To cross, we need to head back to Hattusa, where we'll be caught. We're stuck on this side of the Mighty, unless we go to Santa Fe. There is a bridge there." He then added, "I suggest we skip going to the house and just get food in the barn. The barn doesn't seem to have anyone in it." Indeed, the barn was dark. It was shrouded in a stillness that seemed to imply no human was in the structure.

"You keep food in the barn?" asked Murdo.

"We keep some of the preserved stuff," answered Harold. He looked back at his mother's constant canning with relief now. She spent hours sterilizing the cans and watching over the noisy pressure cooker. They dried, pickled, and canned meat and packed cornmeal into bags that were easy to transport and use. All that hard work would come to good use.

Harold spoke up. "From here, I can sneak to the barn. I can grab enough food to get us to New Lydia without stopping. I think I can get in unseen; it's still Fulldark, and whoever is in the house won't be expecting us."

Greamand and Murdo stayed with the camels in their hidden location a short distance from Harold's barn. Meanwhile, Harold crept toward the barn, his rifle in hand and two saddlebags slung over his shoulder. The barn appeared a black mass against the Illissos sky, and the surrounding pasture was bathed in the blue light of Boreas.

The pasture itself existed because of the extensive irrigation system. His father had put it in when Harold was a little boy. It drew water from the Mighty River. Harold knew that genetic engineering and selective breeding processes had brought grass to Illissos and that another type of grass—still in the works—was said to be exceptionally nutritious and well able to survive the semiarid climate of Illissos. Before being sent to the science labs in New Lydia, the grass had originated in the dry climate of New Mexico; until that grass arrived and was planted here, irrigation was the essential life's blood of all the farms around. The farmers irrigated their crops and the pastures, which fed the animals. To expand the grass was also to expand the irrigation system. Harold, after much hard work, help from the older men, and figuring out how things worked, had added ten acres of irrigated land.

The barn was closer now. Harold didn't see anyone from the house, but he still felt the tremendous unease of being exposed. He felt that every movement, every noise, his very breath would notify the Aviabron humans of his presence. He continued to creep, his heart beating in his throat slowly, ever so slowly toward the barn. He was hunched over, and the saddlebags and rifle felt as though they weighed a ton. Sweat dripped into his eyes, stinging him. Then his foot caught on something, and he fell to the ground, his left hand smashing into a pile of fresh cow manure.

Harold didn't dwell on the fact he'd slipped on a cow pie and had manure spread on his hands and coat because the sound from the fall seemed to Harold to be very loud—loud enough to alert the strangers in the farmhouse. They must have heard something because a beam of light darted from a flashlight held by a solder in front of the house toward the gloomy pasture. Harold stayed down, not moving. If he were spotted, he'd blast away at the soldier and run back to where Murdo and Greamand were, and they'd have a hungry journey to New Lydia. Hungry was better than lying dead on his own field.

The soldier holding the flashlight turned it off and then took a pull on a cigarette. Apparently, Harold hadn't been discovered. The red glow from the cigarette lit the soldier's nose and face. Harold started to move again as the man drew in the smoke. Instead of getting up and creeping again, Harold positioned the bags and rifle on his back and sort of slithered toward the barn across the grass.

It was very hard work. Sweat stung Harold's eyes, and he was out of breath. Once he made it to the barn, he discovered he was masked from those in the house. So he stood up and walked through the livestock door. He heard the breathing and wet warmth from the breath of the livestock therein. The cows often went to the barn without human prodding during Fulldark. He walked in and turned on his red lens flashlight. He passed the jug of kerosene that all farmsteads had for emergencies and went for the pantry where his mother had carefully stored canned food and shelf-stable bread. After loading up the saddlebags with food, Harold shut off the light and felt his way through the darkness of the barn into the pens where the cattle were staying. He had the idea that letting cattle go outside and move about in the pasture would distract the men in the house, making his return to the hide site with Greamand and Murdo that much easier.

He came to the first pen and gently shooed two calves out. They looked at him with confusion and walked to the barn door and the pasture beyond. He continued with the next pen, and the next. Animal noises started to grow, the shuffling of hoofed feet against the barn's floor made a noise loud enough wake the dead. At least to Harold it seemed loud enough to wake the dead. When he got to the last pen, he heard a distinctly human, distinctly female, whimper.

Harold shone his red lens flashlight into the pen. A young woman was half-seated, half-lying down on clean hay. Her hands were bound, and her face was bruised. The left sides of her lips were swollen. She looked at Harold and said, "Don't hurt me."

"I won't," he said. "Who are you?"

"I … I … was brought here by the soldiers," she replied.

Even with only dim red light, Harold could see that she had blue, or at least light colored, eyes and raven black hair. She was wearing a white blouse, dirty, with a long, colorful skirt. A warm, woolen, hooded cloak was nearby.

After a pause, she said, "Can you untie me? These cords are cutting into my skin. It hurts so badly."

Harold pulled out his pocketknife and unbound her. "Come with me," he said. "We need to leave now." Harold grabbed the food-laden saddlebags and headed toward the place where Murdo and Greamand were hiding. The pair weaved through the livestock, which were walking about the pasture in their normal, aimless way.

Harold and the girl were nearly to Murdo and Greamand when a loud shout came from the house. A shot rang out. Harold could hear the bullet as it zinged by his face. As the bullet zipped by, Harold couldn't help but make a small jump and then start running. The girl broke into a run also. When he'd been creeping toward the barn, his rifle and saddlebags had seemed to weigh a ton, but now he hardly felt them. He also calculated with a cold clarity that surprised him afterward that it was best to run and not stop and shoot back. Both Harold and the girl closed on the hiding place, and as they did so, Harold saw Murdo rise up, his rifle in hand. He let off a volley of bullets back toward the farmhouse. One bullet shattered a window; the crashing sound traveled to Harold's ears as he sprinted across the pasture. Harold had a sudden thought that his mother would be furious about the broken window. The house would now fill with dust the next windstorm.

When the two reached Murdo, Greamand said, "Get on the camels," and the foursome headed out into the wilderness at a lurching, camel-run pace. The girl, on the back of Greamand's camel, looked back and let out a scream. "Bavianer!"

Harold looked back. Two of the creatures were lurching toward them at a run. They were dark, lumpy shapes in the gloom, and if they hadn't been moving they'd have been impossible to see. Harold and Murdo turned their camels around and faced the attacking creatures. If they had swords, it would only be a matter of running down the creatures and giving a swing, but they had to hold the rifles steady and shoot. Murdo got his shot off first. It rang true—there was a loud smacking sound as the bullet hit flesh. Murdo's camel panicked as before. Clem was wild with fright, and Harold pulled the reigns tight with his left hand and then raised the rifle, his left hand held the front of the weapon as well as the reigns. Clem breathed heavily.

"Steady!" he said to Clem, but he just as well could have been talking to himself. He had a difficult time drawing a bead on the looming, advancing Bavianer. He fired and missed. Clem gave a leap and galloped away from the Bavianer, which was now a full ten yards closer. Harold decided to wait until it was close enough and then fire point-blank. Clem lurched into the Illissos scrub bushes, causing a horrible crashing noise as the camel crushed the brush. Harold looked back. The Bavianer was only yards away!

The creature made its final lunge, and Harold fired into its torso. He didn't have time to look at the dead Bavianer; instead he concentrated on putting the rifle back on safe and staying seated on Clem, who was now running through the scrubland in total galloping fear. Harold pulled back on the reigns, and after another hundred yards of mad-scramble running, Clem calmed down. Harold felt no great elation for having killed a Bavianer. He just felt relief that they were no longer chasing him. His heart fluttered, and his hands shook.

Greamand assembled the group, and all four got off the camels. "We are now in the great, unsettled wilderness that runs between Hattusa and New Lydia." Greamand pulled out his map, oriented it, and then pointed to the mountains. "That way, across the mountains, and we can make it to New Lydia." Then he turned and pointed north. "That way is Santa Fe. If we go there, our journey will be longer, as we will need to go around the mountains, but we can also take the train." Then, turning to the girl, he asked, "Young lady, what is your name?"

"Leyla," she answered. Her eyes stayed on the ground.

"What caused you to be in this place?" he asked.

"I was brought here by the soldiers," Leyla answered. "They and the Bavianer destroyed my farm." She then looked off into space.

"What can you tell us about the men in the farmhouse?" asked Murdo.

Leyla didn't answer.

"Look," said Murdo with some frustration, "the situation around here is pretty bad. We need you to tell us why you were in that barn."

Leyla only looked down. "I don't want to talk," she said.

Murdo was becoming angry and was reaching to shake her, but Greamand stopped him. "Young lady," he said to Leyla. "Have something to drink." He handed her his canteen and then motioned to the others to come with him.

"Leyla," said Greamand in a voice loud enough for her to hear as they moved away, "we'll just be over here." They had moved to a spot just out of earshot of Leyla if they spoke quietly.

"She's obviously been through some sort of trauma," said Greamand. "We need to stay focused on what to do here. What do we do about her? And do we take the mountain route or go to Santa Fe?"

"I think we should leave her here," said Murdo. "She doesn't seem too bright and will be a drag on us."

"Hold on," said Harold. "It's like Greamand said. She's been through a great deal. I don't think we can leave her here."

They were all speaking lowly. Harold looked over at Leyla. She hung her head and was holding the reigns of the three camels. In the east, the dark blue gloom from Boreas was starting to recede. It was being replaced, ever so slowly, by the light from the sun. Ascent was upon the travelers.

Long shadows started to appear. They stretched out and would very slowly shrink as Ascent became Fullday. As the sun rose above the horizon, it would be like a spotlight. It would be hours before one could look to the east without a blinding glare.

"What if she is a spy?" asked Murdo.

"How could she possibly be a spy?" asked Harold.

"Simple," replied Murdo. "They knew we lost our food by looking at the remains of the mule and its cargo, and they knew you'd go to your farm to get food, and they put her there so we'd rescue her and she can track us."

"How would she track us?" asked Harold.

"She could track us just about anyway. She could have swallowed a tracking device or have one on her clothes," replied Murdo.

Harold looked at Leyla again. She didn't appear interested in what they were saying. She seemed wracked with grief.

"Leave her here," said Murdo.

"Hold on, Murdo," said Greamand. "Your idea is too wildly complex to actually be true. We came to this place and met them here by coincidence. How would anyone from Aviabron know that Harold was with us and this was his farm? I suspect she was kidnapped and brought to that area for evil purposes by the men in Harold's farmhouse."

"What evil purposes?" asked Harold.

"The evil purpose that all young women are at a threat from during war, but I digress," replied Greamand. "We can't turn her loose. She must come with us. If she proves to be treacherous, we can deal with that. Now to the next question—over the mountains, or do we travel to Santa Fe?"

Harold realized what Greamand meant and then felt a great sympathy for Leyla, and he decided that it was best to take her with them, but he held his tongue. There was no point to further the argument when it appeared like the idea that Leyla was coming with them was winning out.

Murdo gave Greamand a very hard look. "I promise that I'll deal with her if she proves false." Then he said, "Mountains. We can be over them quickly if the weather holds, and we won't run into many people who may be a bother up there. And for sure there are no Bavianer. They don't like the hills. I've been over them and know the way."

"Not a bad idea," answered Greamand. "Let's move to a secure spot and stop and reorganize a bit. We should eat some of this food Harold risked so much to get."

Harold realized that he was quite hungry. "That sounds like a great idea," he said.

Murdo quickly agreed, and they headed toward the nearest foothill. Harold looked at Leyla, riding behind Murdo. She hung her head the entire time, not looking at anyone. Murdo looked very unhappy.

As they plodded along on their camels, Harold realized he'd seen those hills his entire life but had never bothered to actually go to them. They loomed larger and larger as the travelers progressed.

Murdo stopped the group and said, while pointing to a draw, "If we go there, we won't be seen from the farm even if we light a fire, and we'll be able to continue on our way with the hills between us and Hattusa's besiegers."

Once the travelers reached a sheltered fold in a hill, the four dismounted. Leyla sat down without saying anything. Greamand looked at her and then said. "It is time to gather some firewood. We might as well have a warm meal for all the effort it took to get the food."

Harold then joined Murdo in breaking off the dried, dead branches and sticks from the native scrub brush, as well as the sticks on the ground. In short order, a small cooking fire was heated, and the group ate.

Leyla looked like she'd been an Orbweek without food, but she didn't express any interest in eating. Harold took the saddle blanket and draped it over Leyla. She looked up and mumbled a "Thanks."

Harold looked at Greamand, and the gray-bearded man locked eyes with Harold in return. Greamand looked at Leyla with an expression of great sympathy and then whisked her off to a quiet, private area surrounded by brush. Harold watched them leave, and Murdo did too. Murdo's face was an expression of worried anger.

"Taking her with us is the right thing to do," said Harold.

"I doubt it. All we're taking with us is risk," replied Murdo.

They said no more while they ate.

After a time, Leyla and Greamand returned. Leyla's gloom was gone, and she ate the heated food.

Chapter 6

THE MOUNTAIN DETOUR

"Leyla," said Greamand, "why don't you tell us about yourself." He then added quietly, "Just like we talked about."

By this time, Leyla was finished with her meal. She put down the empty can, sat up, and began to tell her story. "My family has started a new farm at the fork of two creeks up the valley from Hattusa. Before then, my father worked in New Lydia for other people; his dream was to own his own property. We had an adobe house that was just finished and had planted pasture grass. I had worked with my mother to get a vegetable garden going. Last Orbweek we were having Ascentmeal when, suddenly, two armed men burst into the door followed by Bavianer. The armed men shot my brother before he could stand, and my parents were killed by the Bavianer. The men blindfolded me and took me to another place. I know now it was the barn of Harold's farmstead. There they treated me in a cruel and outrageous way. I was fed some food but left in the pen for some time. I can't say that I heard much, but during Descent, the humans were most excited when they shot some rockets at Hattusa. They kept saying something about making the place a lake and getting rich."

"It seems you've had a terrible go of it, young lady," said Murdo. "It seems you're right, Greamand. This is a bunch of rogues trying to steal the water from the Mighty River. If they pull this off and get Hattusa to surrender they'll have all the time in the world to build a dam. They'd get official help from Aviabron—funding, engineering, security, you name it. They could carry in the building materials by Zeppelin in no time at all. They could even send in robots to carry out most of the work."

"Indeed," said Greamand.

Through this conversation, Harold couldn't help noticing just how stunningly pretty Leyla was. Her eyes were large and azure blue. He kept staring at her. It felt like a compulsion. Every so often, she would look back at him. During these moments, Harold's heart would skip a beat, and he would look away, embarrassed by his inability to not marvel at Leyla's jewellike eyes.

"I think it's time to start to discuss the plan to get over the mountain," said Murdo.

Harold couldn't help feel a deep uneasiness about going over the mountains, but in the excitement of the gun battle and Bavianer chase, he hadn't really been able to say anything. Now he said, "Did we really say we are going over the mountains? I think we should talk about this a bit more."

"I thought the matter was settled," replied Murdo, "but I'll dispense with your misgivings." The way he said *misgivings* seemed a bit condescending, but Harold decided to listen and not argue the point. "I've been through the mountains before," Murdo continued. "It's a bit of a tough slog, but there is fodder and water for the camels if they even need it, and the hills are largely free of Bavianer."

"It's got to be pretty cold through the mountains though," said Harold.

"But it will be much quicker to go this way," answered Murdo. "Look at the map here." Murdo grabbed Greamand's map and spread it on the ground. He pointed to an area that appeared to be less steep than the other places. "This area, this route, it's not as good a pass as one would hope, but if we take it, we shave off two days to New Lydia. We'll be crossing during Ascent and Fullday. We won't be in the dark and the cold at all. I usually try and make it through time of light when I am running sheep. And as I've said, Bavianer don't like hills."

It seemed simple enough to Harold, but he was still worried. He took a breath and said, "What happens if one of the sudden snowstorms comes upon the mountains? In school, there are all sorts of warnings about the sudden storms. Don't get caught out in the mountains, they say."

"School?" stated Murdo a bit contemptuously. "What they say in school is overrated. Most warnings from school are there to control you, make you sit still in class."

Greamand looked at Murdo carefully and said, "This plan appears easy, but storms still are a problem—school warnings or no. What if, let's say, the unthinkable happens and there is a snap snowstorm?"

Harold looked at the sky. The sky was bright blue and clear—completely cloudless. Boreas looked down upon them all like a massive blue eye.

"The Santa Fe Shepherds Guild has some shelters out there," replied Murdo. "If there is snow, we can hold up there for a while and then continue on when the weather clears. This area has been traveled before."

"Have you ever stayed in the mountain shelters during a storm?" asked Harold.

"No," replied Murdo, "but I've been out in the snow on this moon many times. I've never lost a sheep due to the weather." He paused and then pointed to the map again, drawing his finger from the point where they were currently stopped toward Santa Fe. "All that area is Bavianer habitat. Not only will it be a longer journey but a far more dangerous one."

"No more dangerous than what we've had so far," replied Harold. "Also, might most of the Bavianer be surrounding Hattusa? They can't be everywhere at once. If we go to Santa Fe, we might as well have made it to New Lydia. It might be as easy as making a phone call from there."

Greamand made a sigh and then said, "It might not be that easy. It will take just as long to get to Santa Fe from here as to New Lydia, and we really need to get to New Lydia. The problems come down to these: The New Lydians might not send any aid from a phone call. They'll need a direct appeal from a person. The three cities of the Ancient Faith don't cooperate so easily. They might even think the call is a prank, as the call won't be coming directly from the Hattusa mayor's office. Additionally, the high priestess at Santa Fe won't cooperate with me whatsoever. She holds great power in that town, and while I doubt she will stop me from passing through, she could use any excuse to make things more difficult for me."

"It's settled then," shouted Murdo. "Over the hills it is!"

The group headed out. To Harold's delight and surprise, this time Leyla decided to ride behind him on Clem. The three camels pointed their noses toward the hills and plodded on.

From here on, there would be nothing more to do but put one foot in front of the other, uphill and down, until they got to New Lydia. As they moved along, the sky grew dark, although the sun was slowly, ever slowly, rising in the east toward its Fullday position. At one rest break, Harold looked up at the blue giant that was Boreas, and he found it to be hidden behind a layer of gray clouds. Everyone else saw the same thing. Murdo frowned but didn't say anything.

The group continued to travel uphill; the camels obediently continued to plod. Harold gave thanks that his camels were so surefooted. They were specially bred for the terrain and climate of Illissos. Harold could feel the air thin out as they gained altitude. It seemed like the air didn't fill his lungs, and he had to take in more breaths.

The gray clouds continued to darken. The air became sharp and cold. Leyla buried her face and hands into Harold's back. She was only dressed in the clothes she'd been captured in, while the men were equipped with warm jackets and other cold-weather gear. Harold was impressed by how tough Leyla was; she wasn't complaining at all, although she must be terribly cold. Soon, small, powdery flakes of snow began to fall. When the snow began to sting Harold's face, he glanced over at Greamand. The old man's face was nearly green. He was gulping for breath.

It was then that Harold realized that Greamand's age was catching up to him. Greamand, faint from the thin mountain air, started to slip off of his camel, but before he could tumble to the ground, Leyla dismounted from Clem and steadied Greamand.

While Harold, Greamand, and Leyla were stopped, Murdo was continuing to move forward. The flying snow increased; it was being blown directly into Harold's left ear, and each powdery flake had its own special sting.

Harold looked over toward Murdo. He seemed immune to the struggle around him, his Highland Scots ancestry seemed to steel him from the conditions of thin air and biting snow and cold. "Murdo!" Harold shouted, "Murdo! Murdo!"

For a second Harold was afraid that Murdo was going to continue on, and vanish in the swirling snow, but before Murdo did vanish, he stopped and looked back. Harold shouted at him. "Greamand is sick, and this cold is freezing Leyla. We must find shelter!" Harold's words had to go against the wind, which was now howling like an angry Bavianer.

Murdo stopped and looked around and then answered with a certainness that was born of experience. "We are near a rock pen, one of the Shepherds Guild shelters that is set up to protect sheep from these storms. I will lead us there; we can wait this out."

Murdo led the group through the snow, uphill. As they reached the crest of the hill, Murdo made a turn left, and they went into a depression. Inside the depression were two stone walls that intersected to form an X. "I set this up so that sheep and shepherd could be shielded from the wind no matter what way the wind was blowing."

The group then went to the part of the X shielded from the wind and sat down. The camels also lay down. Illissos camels were bred from the type of camels found in Central Asia, and their fur helped them stay warm in the cold. Murdo grabbed a blanket and wrapped Greamand and Leyla together in it. "Harold, grab some firewood—from over there." Murdo pointed to a pile of precut wood with a side of kindling and tinder.

Harold and Murdo assembled the wood to make a fire, while Leyla peeked out of the blanket. The wind howled. Harold had to remove his gloves to light the fire with a cigarette lighter Murdo provided. The cold made his hands numb, and he had a very difficult time getting the fire lit. After what seemed like an eternity, a yellow ribbon of flame peeked through the pile of wood and then went out. With a curse, Murdo added more tinder, and then Harold removed his gloves and lit the tinder again. It was cold, frustrating work, but finally a flame emerged that was self-sustaining.

With that chore finished, Murdo and Harold moved away from their frosted companions so they could talk in private, but they still kept near the fire. There wasn't much more they could do for Leyla and Greamand except let them warm up.

"We'll need to wait it out," said Murdo. All the confidence from before was not present in the expression on Murdo's face. Instead, his face seemed neutral, as though the changing conditions were weighing on his mind. "The blizzard is tough. I underestimated the power of the weather."

Immediately, Harold was filled with anger. *What do you mean underestimated the power of the weather!* he thought. He'd warned against this route. He thought about stomping off, but then where would he go? Instead, he said over to Murdo and, with as much calm humor as he could muster, he said, "I should say, I told you so."

"You could say that," replied Murdo, "but this is a setback while taking this course of action. We could just as easily have had a setback going the way to Santa Fe."

Harold was calmed but not fully impressed by that line of reasoning, and so he said, "How tough will it be to continue on in the snow?"

"We'll wait until the snow stops," replied Murdo.

"No, I mean how hard will it be to travel with the snow on the ground?" said Harold.

"Oh," replied Murdo. "Not too hard. Illissos camels can travel through snow. I'm sure you've done that before."

Harold detected a bit of uncertainty in the reply, and he shook his head no. Before becoming trapped in a shelter on a mountain during a blizzard, he'd never taken the camels through snow. He wasn't sure that Murdo was right. Instead of arguing, though, Harold reasoned that he needed to see the conditions when the blizzard let up before he said anything.

Murdo continued, "The big thing will be to make sure we don't get lost in the mountains, as the terrain could look different when it is shrouded in the white stuff."

There wasn't much more to say. The group took the blankets and sleeping rolls from the saddles and slept, out of the wind near the fire. Ascent was normally the time for sleeping anyway, and they were all pretty tired. The blankets they had were quite warm. The blankets were very advanced technology, and as they were sheltered from the wind and near the fire, they slept in relative warmth, though Harold dreamed he was being pelted by cold, icy rocks. He figured later that the dream was a response to the rocky ground on which he'd slept. At Fullday, he was sore all over but well enough rested.

Also, at the start of Fullday, the storm was over, but the mountains beyond were white with snow. Greamand looked at the mountain, his face ashen white; his breathing seemed labored. It looked to Harold as though Greamand had aged ten years. Leyla looked at the mountains from underneath a blanket she'd wrapped around her head and body and shuddered.

"We need to look at the map," said Harold to Murdo.

Murdo reached in the saddlebag where Greamand's map was normally kept. His hands darted around the inside of the bag, and he then looked through all the other bags. After a fury of searching, he said, "The map is gone." Murdo looked at the mountains ahead. He let out a whistle. "I wonder if we can continue on this way. Without the map and with so much snow, we may need to turn back and get to New Lydia by way of Santa Fe." It appeared to Harold that Murdo's confidence in crossing the mountains had become buried under the snow. It was one thing to believe it was possible to cross snowy mountains when one was sitting around a campfire with a full belly; facing the circumstances in reality was an entirely different thing. The immediate area was blanketed by nearly a foot of snow, and the cover could well be deeper farther on.

"Haven't you been across the mountains before?" asked Greamand. His voice was unsteady and his breathing was still hard.

"I *have* been across these mountains before," replied Murdo.

"Can you guide us without the map?" Greamand asked.

"Possibly. The problem, though, is that the landmarks are blanketed in snow. All the mountains will look different from when I saw them before," replied Murdo.

"It won't be that much different though," replied Greamand. His voice was raspy, and his words were like old, thin paper instead of the forceful, confident words he'd used with the mayor's secretary in Hattusa.

"Look," replied Murdo, "we don't need to continue on this way. I know that I'm the one who pushed for us crossing the mountains as a shortcut. I'm the one who thought we wouldn't get a snap snowstorm, but I was wrong. Farther ahead lie very dangerous conditions. We should turn back and go to Santa Fe."

Harold looked at Leyla; she wore her blanket like a shroud, and only her blue eyes peeked out. Murdo's face wore an expression of worry. He looked at Greamand and continued, almost in a pleading voice, "Why are you so keen on going across the mountains now? We are only about a third of the way across. The rest of the way is pretty perilous. We *might* face Bavianer on the way to Santa Fe but we *will*

snow of the mountains. In the low elevations, the sun's heat lingered around. The air was much thicker too. Greamand no longer looked as though he was gulping for breath, and he was starting to recover. Leyla had folded the blanket that she had hitherto been shrouded in, and it was returned to its place on the saddle. When Leyla caught Harold looking at her, she gave a slight smile and looked away.

"We'll its Santa Fe then," said Murdo. "We'll need to handrail along the mountain range until we get there. In Santa Fe, we can take the train or continue on overland to New Lydia."

Greamand looked very unhappy. "Santa Fe," he said with an ominous tone of voice. He sighed and said again, "Santa Fe … they see things differently there. Don't expect much help in that fair city."

Chapter 7

THE MAN WITH THE FLASHLIGHT

Ever the shepherd, Murdo led the way toward Santa Fe. "From here we just need to have the mountains to our left and Boreas in the sky to our front," shouted Murdo.

And so they pressed on. Harold was on Clem with Leyla. The travelers didn't travel in a single file; instead, one would pull ahead, and another would fall behind. Clem was the fastest camel, so Harold and Leyla tended to be ahead, but Harold was never comfortable being in the lead, so every now and then, he'd slow Clem down and let Murdo pass. In the abstract, Harold knew that all they needed to do was travel north, keeping the mountains to their left, but as they plodded along, and Santa Fe didn't come into view, Harold became uneasy. Harold had never been here before, and without familiar landmarks or any other prior reference, he had no idea how long the journey would be.

There was also the gathering twilight to consider. Fullday was over, the sun low on the horizon. The bluish twilight would soon arrive again. They were once again in rough Bavianer country. Scrub brush and hard, pebbled desert sand made up the terrain. Occasionally, they had to stop and look for a decent place to cross a dry or somewhat muddy creek bed. These obstacles proved to be a tiresome nuisance. During one crossing, the travelers had to dismount, and as they navigated the steep, walled ditch, Harold noticed something like a Bavianer out of the corner of his eye. He quickly grabbed the red lens flashlight and pointed it at the area, but there was nothing. *Perhaps I am dreaming,* he thought.

The first stars appeared in the sky, and Descent officially started. "That one is Canopus," said Greamand, pointing to a star. "And that star is Zephyros, although it isn't really a star; it is a planet in our solar system. It's too hot there for life. We sent a probe to film the surface, and we got some good photographs before the probe became stuck in a puddle of liquid lead."

"How did we send a probe?" asked Leyla.

"A mobile rocket launcher was sent via the spaceport to New Lydia and launched from there," answered Greamand.

As they continued to travel, the camels started walking upon ground that was no longer desert pebbles. Instead it was soil, though mostly grass free. The native scrub brush was intermittently growing throughout "This is good earth, and this area needs to be seeded with pasture grass," said Murdo. "The grazing frontier doesn't advance quickly enough or far enough. I bet the soil here looks really rich, and it could support the best of grass."

"It is certainly a good project for one of the cities or another," said Greamand. "One of the key purposes of government is to support enterprise. I don't think it would be too much effort to get seeds out here."

Harold nodded in agreement. "They could hire out the farm kids for planting in these places. The pasture grass grows so slowly. We are always concerned we'll run out. It is better than before, though. It was so much work for my father to plant the pasture on my farm." Harold thought of the strangers now encamped in his farm, eating the hard won food, using the electricity, taking his stuff, and it filled him with anger. And it wasn't just that; such evil men were threatening Harold's mother and sisters. He wondered if Hattusa was still holding. Then, putting away his terrible thoughts, he continued, "The big question is water. It's always water here. If the Mighty River becomes diverted, no plan to plant grass will work."

"Indeed," replied Greamand with a sigh, "there are also people, governments, tribes, and the like that earn a great living by stealing the produce from the hard labor of others. Our people settled here to get away from such forces; it seems that they have arrived here. One must be ever vigilant."

After a cycle of rest, plodding, walking, plodding onto the ever-deepening blue twilight that made up so much of an Orbweek, Messenger Platoon Six happened upon a patch of pasture grass. The luxuriant carpet of grass started from a straight edge boundary and then blanketed over a rise about a hundred meters away. It was, Harold realized, a man-made pasture. "Hello," said Murdo. "We could be getting close to Santa Fe."

"We need to let the camels get a mouthful. They haven't eaten in a while, and the mountain trip took a bit out of their energy," said Harold. "I don't see any houses or people. Perhaps this is a project from Santa Fe, like what we were talking about."

"A prestaged pasture," said Greamand.

The group dismounted. "I could stand a bit to eat myself," said Leyla.

The canned meals were brought out of the saddlebag, a fire was started, and the meals were heated. The camels' saddles were removed, and Harold hobbled them so they wouldn't be able to stray too far.

As they ate, Murdo asked, "Greamand, how is it that you know so many people in high places? Mayor Winchurst of Hattusa knew you and altered his schedule, during a siege even, to hear you out. You seem to understand people; you are educated. What brings you to the far frontier of Illissos?"

"I was once an up-and-coming priest of our ancient faith," Murdo answered.

Harold, who had been looking into a saddlebag to take an accounting of the food, stopped and listened.

The entire group leaned forward. "What do you mean, once?" asked Murdo.

"A priest cannot allow his personal failings to interfere with his office. Mine did," said Greamand in a matter-of-fact way. "I was cast out. There were a great many priestesses who disliked me before my failings became known, and they moved against me very quickly. I never stood a chance at my disciplinary hearing."

"What was your failing?" asked Murdo.

"A sad secret," replied Greamand. "I regret it wasn't a sweeping idea of reformation, although I expressed some concerns over the actions of a group of priestesses and how they were conducting business before my failing was discovered. Indeed, my failing was likely known by all in power and only became a problem after my concerns were expressed. But I digress. The logical endpoint of their developing philosophy seemed to be a dead end to me. My career and failings are irrelevant, but the philosophy I was concerned with is still a problem. Philosophy is everything, ideas have consequences, and the pen is mightier than the sword. Ideas can be used for good or ill."

"That was an evasive answer," said Murdo. "I take it you won't say."

"Correct. The particulars of my excommunication are forbidden to be spoken of. I suppose that is a blessing," said Greamand. Then he added after a thought, "It also makes for ugly speculation. I left New Lydia and wandered due to the speculation." Greamand looked off into the distance of the blue twilight.

"You keep saying priestesses," said Leyla. "What about the priests?"

"It was mainly several priestesses who brought charges against me, but some of the seminarians who supported my adversaries where men," replied Greamand. He then added, "Those seminarians are now priests themselves. They'll no doubt go far in the priesthood. There was a bit of a generational conflict in my banishment hearings, but it seemed that the older men who lead our faith are more tolerant of my differences, my shortcomings. Recently, cadres of women have moved into positions of leadership, and they don't tolerate my peculiarities at all. Notice that Santa Fe and Hattusa have women serving most religious functions. It used to not be that way."

"So," said Murdo with a little laugh, "do you think our Ancient Faith has become nothing more than a sewing circle for nagging harridans?"

"Ha!" replied Greamand with a smile. "It is a bit more complicated than that, though. Officially, I was cast out due to my failings, but the question comes down to theology. You see, our Ancient Faith has taken hold only among a small group of people and their descendants, even though it claims to be universal. The ideas of the faith haven't jumped to alien species, but the theological questions about universal application of the Ancient Faith to sentient or near-sentient beings still pulls at a large core of our religious leaders. For some reason, it is mostly the ordained women who believe that the Ancient Faith applies to all beings, near sentient or not, in all circumstances. They feel that that their feminine insight and nurturing ways can eliminate the terrible tensions created when aliens like Bavianer meet with more advanced humans. They feel that the hostile attitudes toward the Bavianer are caused by an internal sin on our part, not by our reaction to the behavior of the Bavianer themselves. I feel that might not be correct, but those ideas have proven to light a fire through the establishment of the Ancient Faith, and the women of the clergy are its most fervent adherents."

Just then, Harold couldn't help but yawn greatly. The exhausting travel and stress was getting to him. Being on the grass made him think he was back home. The stress and worry about being in the open in Bavianer country was being replaced by the feeling of blissful sleepiness.

Greamand looked at Harold and then at Leyla. "You two look exhausted. It's certainly been a long Fullday. I suppose disagreements about theological points make the eyelids heavy."

All this time, the people of Messenger Platoon Six were talking around a campfire just as though they were still in the wild. Had they been less tired and scared and had they not lost the map, they would have realized that they weren't just close to Santa Fe as Murdo had supposed; they had arrived right in the middle of the band of the Santa Fe District's productive farm settlements just outside the city itself, although they were still on the edge of the wilderness. They didn't realize that they'd parked their small caravan and started a small campfire on someone else's property.

Suddenly a stab of bright, white light illuminated the circle of travelers. Murdo reached for his rifle and pointed it at the man holding the flashlight. "Go easy, mister. We're armed." Murdo said these words with a fierceness that shocked Harold back into immediate wakefulness.

Harold and Greamand grabbed their rifles also. The camels stood up in excitement, and for several seconds, there was a blurred confusion of noise and motion.

"I'm unarmed!" said the man with the flashlight in a voice that showed no fear. "If you pirates shoot me, you'll be hanged for sure in Santa Fe. What are you doing with your camels eating my grass? I pay so much in tribute to a Bavianer pack I can't afford to let your animals eat for free."

Harold instantly understood the man's concern. Harold worked hard to plant, support, and increase his pasture on his patch of Illissos. He lowered his rifle and pushed down Murdo's raised weapon with a gentle, sure pressure and then said, "I apologize. We had no idea that this was private property. We are on an errand from Hattusa and have traveled a long time. When I saw this field, I emphasized to the others we should allow our camels to graze." Harold knew he could de-escalate the situation, and he figured that a calm voice would help.

"We are moving on shortly regardless," Harold continued, slowly. "Your grass won't be destroyed by our three camels."

"What is this you say about tribute to the Bavianer?" asked Greamand. He held his rifle pointed downward, in a calm manner. Harold realized that Greamand was also working to smooth the situation.

The man with the flashlight relaxed. He shone the light onto the ground at everyone's feet. Harold could see the tension of the situation easing up a bit. The man replied, "I moved to this section of land after I lost my job in New Lydia. I was given some start-up capital from Santa Fe to move to this district, provided I built a house and planted pasture grass and a crude irrigation system. It has been tough, but I'm making do. The wife and kids are fed at least. Then one day, the priestess at Santa Fe preached a sermon that encouraged support for the Bavianer. Again, I'm from New Lydia, not this part of the frontier; supporting the Bavianer seemed a good idea. I thought this idea would bring immediate goodwill between humans and Bavianer."

"Did it?" interrupted Harold. "We have traveled a long way through this area this last Fullday and Descent, and we haven't had any trouble. We only have trouble in Hattusa."

"Yes there is trouble," replied the man with the flashlight. "But it is different than the open warfare of before. It is now law for those of us who were relocated to give a tribute of food and milk to the Bavianer. But the tribute is not the worst of it. Another settler family had their young daughter killed by Bavianer. We tracked down which particular Bavianer did the killing and reported it to the high priestess and the news media in Santa Fe, but the story was not reported, and nobody in the city cared."

"You mean to say that you pay the Bavianer and they still attack? Are there sieges?" asked Leyla.

"We haven't had a siege, but I lose livestock all the time; that's in addition to the tribute." The man with the flashlight kicked at a rock on the ground. "This situation is really an outrage. I can't help but feel that I was duped by the high priestess. We are alone and voiceless. I am a slave for vicious, unproductive beasts so that the priestess in Santa Fe can tell everyone that her enlightened policy keeps down swarms and sieges."

"What is the name of this priestess?" asked Greamand, his eyes narrowing.

"Shazeef," said the man with the flashlight.

"I might know her. Grim face? Thin and tall with dark, somewhat red hair?" asked Greamand.

Harold knew that Greamand knew the high priestess of Santa Fe. The ex-priest was asking a question he already knew the answer to, to see if he could find out something he didn't already know from this stranger.

"Yes," said the man with the flashlight.

Leyla took a breath and started to speak. Harold noticed that her voice had a melody to it. Harold wished he could listen to her laugh or sing for hours and hours. But in the gathering twilight of Descent, her words were every bit as dark. "These sieges are pretty bad. We have one at Hattusa right now."

"I've heard," replied the man with the flashlight. "Don't expect us to come to your rescue in Santa Fe." The man with the flashlight's voice made a quiver of anger, and he continued, "I'd almost rather have a siege. Then at least we could manage the conflict through a decisive, victorious battle. What we have is constant, low-grade conflict."

"Murdo, don't you live in Santa Fe?" asked Harold. "Do you know anything about Santa Fe politics? What is going on here?"

"I live in the Santa Fe District," answered Murdo, "and I only do things with the Shepherds Guild in town," he answered. I live closer in to Hattusa. I've never seen the high priestess, and I'm mostly out on the range with the sheep."

The man with the flashlight continued. "I have to leave out the food soon. It goes in a special container and is scanned by a sensor and chip to make sure that I don't put poison in it. I'd really like to put poison in that food one day."

"I don't understand," interrupted Greamand. "It wasn't too long ago that there were no Bavianer around the settled farmlands at Santa Fe. Out in the wild, they're still around, but I remember that no Bavianer had been seen for a long time. When did they come back?"

The man with the flashlight shrugged. "Hell if I know. I only know that the amount of food that we must give up to the Bavianer seems to always increase. This area seems more dangerous now. We aren't unarmed—I have a rifle in the house—but we are, in a way, disarmed, in that we can't do anything ourselves."

"That I don't get," said Harold. "Why can't you shoot them if they come on your land?"

"I don't know," said the man with the flashlight. "I suppose it would be unseemly socially. If I got caught I think I'd wind up in jail in less than a minute. I think I'd even be in prison if I was rightly defending myself when they were trying to climb through a window of my house."

"Do you have a map?" asked Murdo, changing the subject. "We've come a long way, and I'm not sure exactly where we are."

"I don't have a map, but I can point the way to Santa Fe, if that is where you're headed," replied the man with the flashlight. The beam of light from his flashlight cut across a wooded area. Harold could see the head of a trail about three hundred yards off, and he wondered why he hadn't bothered to really look around when they'd arrived at the pasture and decided to camp out. To the right of the flashlight beams were dark structures—the outbuildings of a farm. "Just follow that trail," said the man with the light. He then laughed, just a little.

The laugh was unnerving.

The group mounted up and started toward the trail, but before they made the wooded trail, they passed one of the outbuildings—a shed. The shed was obviously the property of the man with the light, and around it were the regular items one finds in an outbuilding—garden rakes; a mechanical weed-pulling robot, which was covered in mud and seemed not functional; and a small jug. Leyla stopped Harold, looked to see she wasn't watched by the man with the light, and then slipped off Clem to grab the jug. Before Harold could say anything, she was back on Clem.

"Shhh, it's kerosene," Leyla said.

"Why did you take that?" asked Harold.

"I don't ever want to wait so long for a fire to start like in the mountains," replied Leyla. They entered the trail and the wooded area.

"Isn't that stealing?" asked Harold.

"Yes," replied Leyla, "but I don't care. I've been through enough, and I don't think Mr. Flashlight will notice it missing."

Chapter 8

THE DARKENED TRAIL TO SANTA FE

Messenger Platoon Six guided the three camels along the trail. Greamand took the lead, and Harold and Leyla rode on Clem in the rear. The trail was a hard surface made of packed gravel that was easy to walk across. It cut through a forest. Harold had never seen so many trees in one place before. Only it wasn't a natural forest, where the trees grow haphazardly. This forest was a deliberately planted forest, in which the trees were planted in a pattern, with eight feet of space between each tree. The trees were beyond saplings now, but they weren't big. Each tree trunk was about a foot's thickness across.

Despite the artificial nature of the forest, somehow it still had a dark, wild feel. A wind kicked up, and the branches of the trees made a scraping rustle. Clem gave a snort.

"Steady Clem," said Harold.

Descent was in full swing here; the sun was low; and, in the trees, the changing light conditions only made the forest darker and gloomier. Harold couldn't help but feel a deep sense of danger.

"Greamand," asked Murdo, "have you been here before? To this forest, I mean."

"No," replied Greamand. "I've haven't been to Santa Fe for many years. This seems to be a new, man-made nature park. What bothers me is that there were once many farms all around Santa Fe. It should be a garden, not a forest. Why would the city government, or anybody for that matter, plant a forest here?"

As if to emphasize his point, a ruined farmhouse appeared on the group's left. The roof was gone from the structure, and the brick walls were partially standing. It seemed there was no glass in the windows, but it was difficult to really tell in the twilight.

"What do you think about the man with the flashlight?" asked Leyla. "He gave me the creeps. He has all sorts of complaints about the Bavianer but didn't seem to really want to do anything to help us. The way he laughed when we left …" Her words trailed off.

"Yes," said Harold. "I got a very strange vibe from him too."

Somewhere in the dark forest, a twig snapped.

"It seems," said Murdo, "we don't really know who to trust."

"Trust none in Santa Fe," said Greamand. "Here the Ancient Faith is practiced a bit differently than elsewhere."

"Speaking of that," said Harold, "isn't there a prayer that the Great Dissenter said, when the faithful moved from England to New Mexico so that they could travel safely?"

"There is," said Greamand, "though I doubt the prayer will help."

"Say it anyway," said Murdo.

Greamand took a breath and then said:

"Great gods of humankind,
Be kind, as you find us here
On our way, full of fear;

91

Make our enemies steer quite clear."

Harold had always found that prayer a bit childish, but now, in the dark forest, it made sense that the Great Dissenter had come up with a simple rhyme one could say when traveling through hostile lands.

Another twig snapped. Harold pointed his red lens flashlight toward the sound, but he saw nothing in the red light. The forest was still.

"Greamand," asked Murdo, "why do you not think that that prayer will work?"

"I've found that prayer doesn't seem to do anything," replied Greamand. "I've been trained as a priest and have memorized all the official prayers in the Prayer Annex of the Sacred Scriptures, but it seems that things happen or don't happen regardless of any incantation."

"I suppose that lack of faith helped you get cast out of the priesthood," said Leyla.

"No, not really," replied Greamand. "I've met many priests who have little faith. I've also met many priests who seemed to take to the job for a desire for worldly wealth and power. No, but I've always wondered why our people have put forth so much effort to worship the gods of all humanity when these gods are so hidden and silent. Why did we have the plague twenty years ago? Why didn't the gods intervene to help us? Why did the generation of the Great Dissenter see visions and have so many miracles that helped them while we here, who have created a society based on the Ancient Faith, have so many troubles?"

"I don't think there is going to be a heaven on Illissos," replied Harold.

"I don't think so either," replied Greamand. "But in all my travels, in all my study and prayer and work, I've never been able to see any aspect of the divine. We are on our own when there is real trouble." Greamand continued, "I can't seem to lose my faith entirely, though. The problem is, if one eliminates the gods of all humanity, or the Supreme Being as they are often collectively called, a person replaces that being with something else, and that something else winds up a silly parody of the original. Once you see the concept, you don't unsee it."

"What do you mean?" asked Murdo.

"Oh, like Lenin's Tomb in the Soviet Union," answered Greamand.

"The what union?" asked Harold.

"It was an empire on Earth in the twentieth century," answered Greamand. "It lasted about seventy years or so. What was unique about it was that the father of the empire, a man named Lenin, 'killed' metaphorically their version of god, and the society officially had no religion. The leaders of that empire then replaced their god with Lenin himself after he died. His body, or a wax figure, was used as a sort of idol for many years. The Soviet people worshiped his body, or the wax figure representing his body, for the entire time the empire lasted. The Soviet citizens traveled to his tomb like religious pilgrims. The empire's theology, called Communism, was a sort of religion; it had saints, devils, prophecies, and a vision for a heaven, though in the here and now, not the afterlife. It was the same thing with the golden calf."

"What was the golden calf?" asked Leyla.

Greamand answered, "I don't really want to get too deep into historical theology—I had to study it so hard that I don't feel like repeating it—but it is like Lenin's Tomb. A group of ancient Earth people created a golden calf when their leader was off getting divinely inspired laws by one of the gods of humanity. The golden calf was a ridiculous, mute idol, but the laws that their leader got from that particular god of humanity continue to be used in some form or fashion today."

By this time, the sun was just over the western horizon. It shone like a spotlight. Instead of making the journey through the woods easier, it made things more difficult to see. The sun's brightness made looking toward the right side of the trail too difficult, and on the left side, there was a gloomy, dark sky. The shadows cut across the trail, and it was difficult for a person's eyes to truly adjust. Descent was normally the time for sleeping, and Harold could feel himself drift off to sleep. Had they not been interrupted, Harold would have suggested to the platoon that they sleep on the comfortable pasture grass. He shook himself awake. Leyla, riding behind Harold, had put her head on his back, and she appeared to be sleeping.

They plodded along. Harold noticed another ruined building. Its roof had caved in, and a small tree was poking out of the center of the building. Then suddenly, the oil refinery smell of Bavianer filled his nostrils. Clem gave a snort, and Harold shouted "Bavianer!" as loudly as he could.

But before the word really left his lips, there was a horrible snarl, and with a flurry of dark fur and motion, Greamand was knocked off his camel and the air filled with a horrifying mix of human and Bavianer screams. Murdo gave a shout of surprise and fired off three rounds from his rifle; his camel bucked and snorted. Leyla screamed in panic and slid off Clem, but Harold pulled on Clem's reigns and got control of the camel.

A curious feeling came upon Harold. In the past, when the oil refinery smell of the Bavianer came, a tremendous feeling of fear would rest upon Harold and bring a paralysis to his hands and feet. This time, something different happened. Harold's sense of vision seemed to expand beyond the normal human range, and his mind, which normally ran with the distracting, internal chatting voice of Harold's inner conscious, calmed into a peaceful but laser-like focus on the Bavianer that had just tackled Greamand. Time seemed to slow down. The struggling movement of Greamand and the Bavianer on top looked to Harold to be playing out as though underwater. Harold looked at the exposed back of the neck of the Bavianer and instantly realized just how advantageous a saber was in anti-Bavianer warfare. Had he been equipped with this weapon, he could stay on Clem; ride by the creature; and, with a quick stroke, sever its head and end the fight. However, Harold had a high-powered rifle. If he shot, he risked also shooting Greamand. Clem would also buck when he shot.

Harold looked over to Leyla—who was standing and looking on the scene of struggle with a paralyzed fear. Harold shouted to her, "Leyla! Grab the reins!"

She shook her head, looked at Clem, and took the reins, and Harold slipped off. With his seemingly expanded vision, Harold noticed that Murdo had also dismounted, but he was looking toward the spotlight that was the setting Descent sun. Harold ran toward the Bavianer; it was a massive buck. When he got to a point-blank range, he took a knee—all this took seconds but seemed to take a lifetime—and he fired into the flank of the beast. Instantly, the Bavianer's head twisted, and the creature went limp. Harold pushed the dead Bavianer off Greamand.

"Don't help me. I'm okay," Greamand whispered in voice that seemed to say the opposite. His face was ashen gray. "Help Murdo ..."

Harold looked into the sun, but he had to instantly close his eyes; it was too bright. The Bavianer had taken advantage of this condition and attacked out of the sun. The instant that he looked toward the sun, Harold's expanded vision shrank back to normal, and the sights and sounds returned to their normal speed. Harold's laser-like mental focus also returned to normal, and his ears picked up on the sounds Murdo was making. Harold could hear Murdo's feet shuffle and his heavy breathing.

"They're over there," shouted Murdo. He pointed toward the forest, off the trail.

Harold took his left hand and, with it, blocked the sun. It made seeing a little better. Sure enough, three more creatures, all bucks, were snarling and making a threatening display with their hands and arms at Murdo and the other humans. Murdo fired but missed. Harold raised his rifle, but when his left hand went from blocking the sun to holding the front of the rifle, the spotlight returned, and all he could see was a blinding glare through the rifle's sights. He didn't fire.

"Murdo," shouted Harold, "stay there. I'll go around to the left."

Harold bolted back along the path toward Clem and Leyla. He then stepped off the trail on the western, left-hand side; walked into the forest; and ran, snaking through the trees back toward the three Bavianer. This way, Harold would flank the creatures. The lights conditions remained the dazzling mixture of spotlight, gloom, and shadow. Harold didn't see the Bavianer until he was nearly on them. When he saw the three creatures, he raised his rifle, but the center Bavianer somehow sensed Harold. He sniffed the air and swiveled his head around, and then the beast looked directly at Harold. It made a throaty noise, and the three animals bolted away at a speed too fast for Harold to aim and shoot.

For a second, the forest was quiet and Harold was unsure where the creatures had fled. Harold looked around. A native Illissos hover-bird, not brightly colored but more of a dull beige with dull purple wings, zipped into the space between the trees. It floated still, wings flapping so quickly that they seemed invisible, and then the bird zipped off.

"Harold!" it was Murdo. "Haaarooold!"

"Here!" shouted Harold.

Murdo continued, his voice clear, "If you move forward and to the left, you'll see them. They're in a wrecked farmhouse."

Harold moved in the direction described by Murdo. After just ten tiny steps, a wave of uncertainty gripped him. *Am I going the right direction?* The trees seemed closer in now—taller somehow. Their shadows were dark and sinister. *Am I being led into an ambush?* The sun remained low and blinding.

Harold made ten more steps toward the location Murdo had described. He wanted to stop, to turn and run back to the trail. Then Leyla ran up beside him. She had the jug of kerosene.

"We can burn them out," she said. Her eyes flashed with an angry courage. Her face had an expression that said *vengeance.*

Harold took a few more steps forward, and then a ruined structure came into view. He'd been traveling in the right direction all along. The structure was unseeable until now due to the trees, shadows, and blindingly low sun. It appeared to be a building once used for some sort of light manufacturing. It was rectangular in shape, made of cinder blocks, and its windows held the remains of broken glass.

The roof was rusted metal, and on its left side was a gaping hole with a tree, a small, fast-growing type, growing up through it. The building was by no means large, perhaps forty feet on its broad side.

"Harold!" shouted Murdo. The shepherd was approaching the building from the right, rifle at the ready. Harold waved back and pointed to the thinner side of the building.

"Go there," he shouted, "watch the front door."

"Oh the smell," said Leyla.

"Murdo," shouted Harold, "fire into the window on your side; we'll burn them out."

Without a word, Murdo started to shoot into the building. Harold and Leyla were perpendicular to Murdo's gunfire.

Also wordlessly, Leyla lifted her skirt with one hand to run more easily, and with the other holding the jug, rushed toward the first window on the right of the front door. She poured the kerosene out and struck a match she had taken from one of the saddlebags, and soon a massive pillar of fire reached into the gloomy sky. A noise, an inhuman, screeching howl, a sound like chalk on blackboard or a cat scratching on glass with its claws, came from the inside of the building.

From the window on the left, a Bavianer started to come out. Harold raised his rifle, sighted in on the dark center mass, and fired the remaining shots in his rifle's magazine. With the last shot, the metal clip ejected from the top of the rifle with a *sprang*. Harold reached for another eight-round clip to fire more into the window, but now the dry bedding, or whatever was in the building, had caught fire also, and the whole ruined structure was alight. The inhuman noise coming from within became louder, both more horrifying and pitiable, and then, suddenly, the screaming Bavianer fell silent. A terrible smell, like charred beef mixed with an oily scent, hit Harold's nostrils like a well-placed blow from a fist. But before he could think on the smell further, his thoughts were interrupted by another shot from Murdo's direction. "I got him," Murdo hissed in a savage, angry way. He'd killed the last beast. Murdo then shouted, "Greamand! We must get him help."

The three turned their back to the burning building and made their way to the trail. Harold briefly thought they were lost, but after snaking around a large spruce tree, they were back on the trail. Although Harold had felt that he was fighting a battle in the center of a dark wood, it turned out the entire thing had happened just along the trail's edges.

"Right," said Murdo. "Go right along the trail."

They went to the right, back toward where Greamand was. First they walked, and then Leyla started to run, holding her skirt as she ran. The others followed. Greamand and the three camels came into view. Greamand had propped himself so his back was resting on a tree trunk, and he was holding the reins of Bedouin Bit.

"Are you hurt?" asked Murdo.

Harold could see that Greamand's robes were splattered in blood. "Of course he's hurt," snapped Harold. "Look at the blood!"

Leyla bent down and looked at the ex-priest's injuries. "We need to take him to a hospital. Here, get me some cloth to use as a bandage."

"No!" replied Greamand. "We need to get through Santa Fe without being seen. We must be inconspicuous. Bandage me up as best as you can and skip the hospital visit." Greamand's voice sounded hoarse. His face was pale, and he wobbled unsteadily.

Leyla looked at the other two; she shook her head no, and her eyes were wide and frightened. "He needs major medical assistance. We need to get him to a hospital."

"No hospital until New Lydia," answered Greamand roughly.

"Can we afford it?" asked Harold ignoring Greamand's pleas. He'd heard his mom discuss medical expenses before. Now that adult responsibility seemed to have fallen from the sky and landed on his shoulders, and it gave him worry.

"Look at Greamand," said Murdo. The ex-priest was in and out of consciousness.

"They have to treat you if it is an emergency," replied Leyla. "I'll switch camels and help steady him. We need to get to Santa Fe pronto."

Riding arrangements were adjusted, and Greamand was put on his camel; the three camels with their riders hurried along. The altitude was much lower around Santa Fe than at Hattusa. Harold felt that he could breathe easier. The sky continued on with its darkening blue. It was nearly Fulldark, and Harold's exhaustion returned as before. The gentle rocking of the camel's walk tried to lull Harold into an involuntary sleep. Harold thought of what the people in the cities would be doing. During this part of an Orbweek, Illissos residents were resting. They would get up in a few hours and go about their Fulldark activities under the glow of electric lights. If no more delays occurred, Messenger Platoon Six would make Santa Fe at the start of human wakefulness during the darkest time of the Orbweek.

The trail was starting to dwindle out, replaced with irrigated crops and plants from Earth. There were cottonwoods along the riverbank. Soon, they came upon a road. It was paved with stones in the manner of a Roman road on Earth. It was the first such road that the travelers had seen since their escape from Hattusa. "I know this road," said Murdo. "We can take it in all the way to Santa Fe."

Soon, by the side of the road, small farms appeared. Trees from Earth, mostly Ponderosa pine but some piñon pine trees, also lined the road, and rock walls surrounded the properties. One area housed several camels, and the animals walked up to the wall and peered at the band of travelers as they passed.

Harold looked over at Greamand. He was quiet. His mouth was clamped shut. His face was tight with pain. Every so often, Leyla would whisper something to him.

"We'll get you help soon," said Harold to Greamand. "Hang on."

Murdo took a breath and then said, "Why do you think the Santa Fe government made that forest we just passed through? Why did they let the houses go to ruin?"

"It is habitat," replied Greamand. His voice was a gravely mix of anger, fear, and hurt. "Shazeef made the place for the Bavianer to live right next to the settlers. It's a dead end. The Bavianer will repopulate this area. Mark my words. Soon they'll be in Santa Fe itself. The hopeless impulse to convert the Bavianer to the Ancient Faith is a major part of Shazeef's agenda."

After that burst of anger, Greamand's head slumped. Leyla held him tightly.

Murdo whispered to Harold, "Do you think he is delirious from fever?"

Harold shrugged; he didn't know about such things. He only knew that Greamand needed medical attention.

The road took a turn, and soon, the travelers saw a stone bridge across the mighty river. The stone was colored with the beige that made up the rocks of the mountains of Illissos. It was the grandest thing that Harold had ever seen.

"The bridges at New Lydia are even more spectacular," said Greamand weakly.

As they crossed the bridge, they approached the gate of Santa Fe. A single guard was there, but he didn't stop them. He just looked them over, averted his eyes, and typed on his comms device.

Once in the city, Murdo took the lead, "Follow me. I know the way to the hospital."

Chapter 9

THE SANTA FE ARREST

Harold and Leyla sat in Greamand's hospital room. Several robots, along with human medical staff, had tended to Greamand's injuries. Greamand's forearms were mostly covered with superficial defensive cuts, but the skin on his upper arms and shoulders was flayed and shredded. After the initial flurry of treatment, Greamand was now resting comfortably. Murdo had taken the camels, rifles, and supplies to the public stables in the center of town. While at the hospital, Leyla also had her injuries, inflicted in the barn, tended to. The plan was to allow Greamand to recover enough so they could take the train to New Lydia. The camels were to be stabled in Santa Fe in the meantime.

A robot that looked like a wheeled carriage with a single robotic eye and four mechanical hands and arms moved to change the bandages on Greamand's arms. The robotic eye shone, its earth-tone lights changing from beige to green to rocky gray and then to the Boreas blue gloom tint. These colors relaxed everyone. Harold's eyelids became heavy, and he felt like he was in a trance. As the robot changed the bandages, it made comforting, nonvocal humming noises.

After Greamand's initial check-in and diagnosis, very few humans had bothered to come into the room. A single nurse entered the room. The nurse gave a hard look at Greamand, Leyla, and Harold and scowled. Leyla returned the scowl with the kindest of smiles.

"We've done what we can for him," said the nurse briskly. "All he needs to do is heal. We'll give him pain medication on a schedule."

Leyla and Harold were seated on a row of chairs that had been placed against the wall facing the door in the room next to the hospital bed that allowed families and friends of stricken patients to be near their loved one. The chairs were by no means comfortable. Harold looked over at Leyla. She was still wearing her traveling clothes, and they were dirty. Her bright skirt was looking threadbare and ragged. Harold had his militia coat by his side. He had also not changed, and his clothes smelled like a toxic mix of human sweat and Illissos dirt. The hair on Harold's face scratched and bothered him. The growth of hair on his face hadn't really bothered Harold in a physical way until today. Before it had only bothered him that it wasn't shaved by means of the ritual that would officially mark his passage into manhood. Now his cheeks were a dirty, itchy mess.

Harold's eyelids became heavy again. The lack of sleep, the excitement, and the quiet hospital with its lemon and plastic smell conspired to pull Harold into a sleep. It seemed that he went straight from wakefulness to dreaming in a single instant.

In his dream, Harold was passing through a forest … It was *the* forest, the Bavianer forest. It was dark and gloomy, but every now and then, a brilliant light would stab into Harold's eyes, temporarily blinding him. The forest seemed to go on and on; the ruined human structures in the forest went from tiny homesteader houses spread far apart to more complex buildings, which eventually became entire neighborhoods. Then Harold saw the hospital. It was unkempt and abandoned, and trees grew out of the upper-story windows. A Bavianer was sleeping on the front steps of the hospital. Propelled forward by some unseen but powerful force, Harold was forced to approach the creature. He was swept up the concrete steps and into the face of the animal. The Bavianer looked up at him, and in Murdo's voice it said, "Harold."

"Harold …" In his dream, the hospital shook; there was an earthquake.

"Harold …" And Harold woke up to see Murdo standing over him. "Get up," Murdo said. "Help me get Greamand. We need to go. Santa Fe's high priestess has a warrant for our arrests."

Murdo moved to the bed and started unhooking Greamand from the various wires that connected his body to the sensor machines. Leyla was groggy. Harold took her arm and filled her in on what Murdo had said.

Murdo was nearly in a panic. His eyes were glassy with fear. His fear infected the rest of the group. Harold felt the same dreadful, paralyzing feeling as he had when he'd saddled the camels on the first day of the siege. He willed his hands and feet to move again, remembering that his family was trapped in Hattusa. Harold looked at Leyla; her eyes were wide with fright. "We need to get somewhere, anywhere not in public."

The group shambled out of the room.

"Ahhh," said Greamand. "Slow down. Moving hurts."

The hospital corridor was long. Above, the florescent lights flickered. They made a low, nearly inaudible hum.

Leyla, Harold, and Murdo each made a different suggestion as to how to easily move the injured Greamand. An argument started, but then Greamand said in his authoritarian voice, "Just go around and find a wheelchair."

The three went separate ways. Harold went down the corridor and then took a left. He slowed down, started a walk that was a leisurely pace, which would imply to any nosy authority he was a natural visitor to the hospital, not a wanted fugitive. If someone bothered to notice him and ask why he was dirty, he figured that he'd say that he'd been checking in for treatment and had gotten lost. He passed a hurried nurse who didn't look up at him. He took another left to another long corridor. At the far end of the corridor were two policemen. They wore blue suits, and each wore a blue fez with an emblem of some sort on its front. Harold froze. The two policemen appeared to be searching for someone. They were intensely looking into each room. Harold backed up and returned as quietly as before, but he moved at a very quick pace. When he returned to the door of Greamand's room, he discovered that Leyla had found a wheelchair and she was helping Greamand into it.

"Police," said Harold. "They're in the other wing, and they're looking for something." He then added, "Say, why do they have an arrest warrant out for our arrests?"

Murdo answered, "I don't know if it is a warrant with our names on it, but automatic arrest orders are out for persons matching our descriptions. Apparently, someone got wind that we killed the Bavianer. The police are onto us. I know this because the head of the Shepherds Guild sent me a warning to my e-mail account. I checked it at the public kiosk when I stabled the camels."

"Easy, Greamand," said Leyla after Greamand made a small jump at Murdo's description of the arrest warrant. "Let's head to the exit door on this wing."

"How did the high priestess get word that we'd killed those Bavianer?" asked Harold. He then felt a hot rush of anger. "What did you do besides stable the camels and check your e-mail, Murdo?"

"Are you saying that I reported you?" asked Murdo. His face was angry and hard. "Why would I do that? I'm in with you on our mission."

"Wait," said Leyla seeking to head off a serious argument. "The police probably went to the wrong hospital wing by mistake, which is why Harold saw them over there. They'll figure their mistake out very quickly and come over here. We need to move."

"And besides," said Murdo, ignoring Leyla and still looking at Harold, "it is likely that the forest is covered in sensors. The high priestess is looking to catch any human that causes harm to a Bavianer. Even the flashlight man we met before we got to the forest could have reported us."

Then from down the hall there was a shout. "Hey! You there! Stop!" It was the police.

"This way!" said Murdo. Harold went behind Greamand's wheelchair, and they all scrambled toward a side hall and a door that led outside. The door was made of unbreakable, clear glass. They opened the door by pushing a crash bar on which large red were printed:

EMERGENCY USE ONLY
ALARM WILL SOUND WHEN DOOR OPENS

As they crashed through the door, an alarm sounded, and brilliant strobe light flashes stabbed harsh, bluish light into the corridors. Once outside, the foursome found themselves standing on the upper landing of concrete stairs. Seven steps led down to the street, and there was no wheelchair ramp. To Harold's right was an emergency fire hose. He grabbed it and put it through the outer door handles and quickly made a knot. "It will hold the police for a little while."

"Hurry," said Leyla. "We need to get Greamand down."

"I'll walk down, quicker," said Greamand. He stood up and painfully walked down the stairs. Murdo grabbed the wheelchair and carried it down. Harold and Leyla bounded down the stairs. They were out of the hospital, on a sidewalk, and right next to a small city park with manicured grass and trees. Harold looked up. Boreas was in its place—a slightly different spot in the sky than at Hattusa—and not only was Fulldark over but Ascent was well on the way. They'd lost valuable time in the hospital. The sky was just beginning to become light. The ground remained dark. Visibility was hampered by the twilight that made the residents of Illissos walk carefully.

Then a loud bang came from the door behind them. The police were straining to open the two heavy doors. The knotted fire hose was holding—for now, but they had to move and move quickly. Greamand was back in the chair, and they wheeled him across the park into a residential area. A few turns and the four were in an alleyway. It was dark in the alley—and quiet.

Harold looked at Murdo. "Where can we go?"

Murdo looked down, took a deep breath, and said, "We should go to a restaurant or diner near the train station. We can hide there and then get on the train at the last minute. We won't be conspicuous at a public location where travelers come and go."

"Won't the police be looking for us there?" asked Leyla. "If they know who we are, they'll know we're trying to head out of here. Won't they go straight to the diners near the train station to try to cut us off?"

"Let's keep moving," said Greamand. "We just need to get the camels and get out of here. We need to go independent of the train—less chance for arrest."

"Can you ride?" asked Murdo.

"I rode here after being injured," said Greamand. "It is better being injured and out of Santa Fe than being here and injured in prison. I've told you; they see things differently in Santa Fe than people do in Hattusa. We are in bigger trouble than you may realize."

The four started to walk or roll toward the stable. Greamand was in his hospital robes, and Murdo was wearing clean shepherd's clothing. But Leyla and Harold remained in their dirty traveling clothes. Mud splatter coated Harold's warm militia jacket. They kept to the back streets and alleys. The gloomy conditions helped keep them out of sight. Then they got to a large intersection. Because Ascent is normally the time for sleeping, the two large roads were empty.

"Across this intersection and beyond those buildings is the stable," said Murdo. "When we get the camels, there are a variety of ways to escape the city without being seen."

"Just a second," said Harold. "I'll walk across the street, take a look at what is over there, and then you come when I beckon." Harold had a feeling that crossing the road and seeing what was over there was a good idea. He also suspected that there wasn't anything to worry about and he'd be making a much-appreciated gesture—especially much appreciated by Leyla.

He walked forward, looked at the road, and then darted across. He looked back. Sure enough, Leyla was looking at him with large, expressive eyes. Harold looked at the buildings and went to a corner, expecting to see nothing there. He would then wave everyone forward.

When Harold peeked around the corner of the building what he saw just in front of him were two policemen. Harold felt like his heart stopped. They saw him, and their faces jumped with recognition. Harold realized his description had been given to every beat cop in town. It was over for him now; Harold had walked into a trap.

One of the officers shouted, "Halt!" in a loud voice.

Harold turned to run, but one of the officers took a small cylinder from his belt. It looked a bit like a hollow, black tube, and when he pointed it at Harold, it made a high-pitched screech. Then an electric sensation that seized every muscle into an impossible frozen state gripped Harold. He collapsed to the ground; his legs twitched. He tried to cry out, but that proved impossible. It felt like his arms and torso were being crushed. His eyes filled with tears.

"You're under arrest by order of the high priestess of Santa Fe," said a policeman. The electric grip on Harold slackened just a bit.

Harold looked around for the others through a tear-streaked haze, but they had disappeared, and the police weren't chasing after them. A wave of anger and shame washed over Harold; he'd never been arrested before. An unexpected feeling of resentment also welled up in Harold's chest. He would be in prison while the others were free. Now, he was utterly alone.

Harold was handcuffed and escorted to the police station. Harold was glad it was Ascent and fewer people were on the streets than would otherwise be. He couldn't help but feel enormous shame at being handcuffed and in the custody of the police. He felt disapproving looks (possibly imaginary) from every Santa Fe woman peering from her bedroom windows burn his skin. Harold looked at the emblem on the fez of the policemen. It was an eagle within a star.

In the police station, he was taken to a waiting area and kept in handcuffs. A tall, muscular, shaven headed policeman who looked to be in charge of the shift looked at him and then started to fill out things on a glowing flat-screened device. The policeman had a handsome face, but his nose appeared to be off center, as though it had been broken and never properly reset.

"Go ahead and sit down there, young man," said the bald, broad-shouldered officer. He pointed to a different room that held a long, wooden bench. "I need to finish processing your paperwork." Harold didn't say anything and then sat on the bench. As soon as he did so, the officer closed a door made of iron bars.

In the room was an old television set. The walls were the usual adobe bricks that made up so much of the Illissos building material. The TV was showing some sort of entertainment and political event going on at a Santa Fe studio. Musicians were on a stage. The stage itself was covered in red, white, and blue bunting, and there was a large emblem of the eagle within the star in the center. On the upper left-hand corner of the TV screen was a glowing message: "Live Recording."

Harold normally got pretty bored with singing shows, but with nothing to do while the "paperwork" got done, he watched. The show was the strangest stage act he'd ever encountered. A bald, thin, gray-bearded folksinger played a banjo. Harold had seen this singer before, but he couldn't remember his name. The singer was wearing blue jeans and a paisley patterned shirt. To his left and right were other musicians with guitars. Three women to the singer's left rear were handling the backup harmony.

The old man was from a subsegment of Illissos called folkies, who were into the Ancient Faith but tended to be looser with some of the religious interpretations. Specifically, they liked to smoke an herbal, mind-altering substance. Despite being looser on some areas, the folkies also seemed to Harold to be grindingly preachy. Folkies often wrote songs that purported to be of the people or folk, and the songs ranged from the serious spiritual and traditional, to funny and unserious. In this case, the thin folkie was singing an old favorite called "This Land is Your Land." It originated on Earth, but its lyrics had changed to reflect Illissos geography.

The singers crooned, *"This land is your land; this land is my land, From the Mighty River to the Great Green Glacier ..."*

The song was about the interesting points of Illissos, though it left out the long expanse of scrub, didn't mention Aviabron, and didn't say anything about Bavianer violence whatsoever. But it wasn't the singers of the song Harold couldn't take his horrified gaze from, for behind them were juvenile Bavianer. Incredibly, they were sort of dancing in time with the music. At first, Harold thought that they were tame and docile, like cows, or perhaps trained like the Aviabron Bavianer now surrounding Hattusa. But then he realized that the creatures wore large, thick collars and restraint ropes that anchored them in place.

The concert was the most awkward, patronizing, and unsettling thing Harold had ever watched. The Bavianer were so out of place when it came to traditional Illissos songs. Then one of the Bavianer, a young buck still lacking the silver hair on the front paws of an older buck made a sort of lunge at a backup singer. The restraint held, and the singer's face made a sudden flash of fear. The singer then composed herself and continued to sing. It was only a second, a tiny flinch. But it appeared to Harold that even the musicians on the stage were unsettled by being so close to the Bavianer.

The show wasn't just unsettling; it was stomach turning. The pretty young women singers so dangerously close to the Bavianer dancers gave Harold much unease. Additionally, the distasteful mixing of traditional music and symbols of the humans with a crass political pitch for Bavianer integration was really jarring. Just when Harold was about to turn away from the program in disgust, the camera filming the show zoomed its view inward. The restless Bavianer were cut from the TV's frame of view. The show's view then cut from focusing on the singers to a sort of montage of images as the song reached its climax. The montage showed the famous painting of *the Great Dissenter* on Pendle Hill, followed by an image of the charter *the Great Dissenter* had made when those of the Ancient Faith had decided to travel to Illissos—its large, handwritten script standing out against the yellowed parchment.

A loud buzz interrupted Harold's TV watching. It came from the iron-barred door. "Stand up." The cop with the shaved head marched in. "Prisoner, you stand accused of the hateful murder of Bavianer who are protected by the affirmative rights laws in the Santa Fe Bavianer forests. You will be placed in a single holding cell where you will be fed as normal until your trial. It is best to confess as soon as you can."

Harold was then moved to a single cell and left alone in silence.

***

While Harold was being arrested, Murdo directed the others into a darkened alley away from the street and out of the view of the police.

"Well," said Greamand weakly, "that didn't work. We need to think of something else. Who do you know in Santa Fe that can help us?"

"The Shepherds Guild Lodge is near here," said Murdo. "We need to continue to travel along this back alley and then cut over onto Central Square. We can get sanctuary there."

"Why didn't you think of that before?" asked Leyla.

Murdo paused and then said, "I guess I was too concerned with getting us out of the hospital and out of town. Now that I have my bearings, a better strategy has come to me."

The three traveled slowly. Greamand winced with every jolt in his wheelchair. In a raspy voice, he said, "Painkiller is wearing off."

"We should have grabbed painkillers before we left the hospital," remarked Leyla.

"We didn't have time," said Murdo.

"It can't be helped," said Greamand. "I'll manage."

"Isn't there a prayer for healing in the Ancient Faith?" asked Leyla. "You could say that."

Greamand gave a little chuckle and didn't pray.

The trio crossed Central Square without incident. Murdo pointed to a flat-faced building of Illissos-brown adobe brick and said, "There it is."

They opened the door and entered the building. The walls were decorated with various things associated with sheep. There was a pair of shears on the wall, as well as some sheep hides with long, luxurious wool still attached.

Greamand got up from his wheelchair and plopped down on his back on a leather couch covered in a brown fleece. "Murdo, we need to change clothes; we need to look different in some way. And we need to change and get to New Lydia by train. What is the schedule for departures?"

"You mean leave Harold in jail?" Murdo gasped. "We can't do that."

"We must do that," replied Greamand. "I can free Harold by pulling strings from New Lydia politically if our mission is successful. We need to go; our mission is too important to get held up here."

A man entered the room. He was wearing a smoker's jacket and black, wool felt pants. His outfit appeared tailored. The clothes looked to be deliberately selected to be comfortable and impressive during social calls outside of regular visiting hours.

"Just a second," Murdo said to Greamand. "Hugh MacGregor!" said Murdo. "I'm glad to see you here."

MacGregor looked the ragged-looking strangers over warily.

Murdo held out his hand and shook MacGregor's hand with a special handshake. Murdo then said, "Great brother shepherd, this lowly traveler calls upon you to aid in my distress." Murdo then flashed what appeared to be a hand signal, but Leyla couldn't quite make it out or describe it.

"I can help a traveling shepherd," replied MacGregor in a solemn voice.

"We need to lay low for a bit and then take the train to New Lydia," said Murdo. He then explained the situation—the siege, the forest, and Harold's arrest.

MacGregor's eyes narrowed and his face was expressionless. "You can stay here for a while, but you're in big trouble. You need to know that, politically, Santa Fe is under no treaty with Hattusa and takes on no obligations to help out Hattusa. Additionally, this talk of some conspiracy to direct the Mighty River seems like craziness and rumor spreading."

"Why would it seem like craziness and rumor spreading?" asked Greamand in a dry, firm voice. "I promise you that this conspiracy is not crazy and is ongoing right now."

"We have some caravans to and missionary work with Aviabron," replied MacGregor. "High Priestess Shazeef has a mission of sorts there. Those of Aviabron are not yet of the Ancient Faith. You need to understand that a large portion of the population here is crazy for the high priestess and her ideas. You need to know, the high priestess never seems to do anything wrong in office. She moves from one political and moral victory to another. The local media is totally on her side."

"Have they made any converts in Aviabron?" asked Greamand.

"I don't really think so," replied MacGregor. "I'm not a religious man myself. I just live in a religious society. My focus is business—sheep products, wool, grazing, mutton, lamb chops, leather." MacGregor looked around. "Please excuse me for a second." He went back into a different office.

"This is bad," said Greamand. "Murdo, Leyla, our mission might end here. He might be calling the high priestess now."

Leyla let out a worried sigh and sat down fearfully.

"He wouldn't do that," said Murdo. "I've been given sacred sanctuary by right of the Shepherds Guild. We all swore a sacred oath when we joined." Despite the encouraging, words, Murdo looked worried.

Greamand sat up on the couch, very slowly, and said, "Look, we need to get a comms device and call New Lydia long distance. I doubt very much such a call will get us aid, given how uncooperative the three cities of the Ancient Faith are, but I fear we'll be arrested soon. It is the best we can do with the circumstances as they are. We must do what we can to accomplish our mission."

"Okay," said Murdo. "I'll try and get a comms device."

MacGregor returned. "I have tickets for you on the Fullday train. Is there anything more?"

Leyla breathed out a sigh of relief. MacGregor hadn't betrayed them. At least he hadn't betrayed them yet.

"Can I borrow your comms device?" asked Greamand, using the voice that conveyed authority to the best of his injured ability. "Formally, it is best to deliver letters from the Hattusa mayor, but now I need to contact either the Secular Authority in New Lydia or the high priest."

MacGregor gave a comms device to Greamand. He tried to call several numbers. "All I get are rings. I don't even get an answering machine."

"I'm not surprised," said MacGregor. "Try sending a text message."

Greamand started to type:

> To: High Priest Sadra, New Lydia
> This is Greamand—one time priest of our Ancient Faith. Along with others, I have been commissioned by Mayor Winchurst of Hattusa to plead for assistance.
> The City of Hattusa is besieged by a force of Bavianer and humans from Aviabron. There have been many casualties among the militia. The city's communications assets have been destroyed by precision-guided

munitions. It is my belief that the city
will fall without aid from New Lydia.
I furthermore believe that the city is
besieged in order to divert the water
from the Mighty River to Aviabron.

Please respond via this comms
account.

"Well," said Greamand, "I don't know if that will work
or not, but the message is now delivered. We'll need to see
what sort of response we will get."

After a minute, the comms device made a buzz. "It's the
response," said Greamand.

But it wasn't a response. Instead, it was a message,
which said:

*To keep our society based on absolutes
and avoid apostasy, all calls to New Lydia
Religious Authorities must be approved by
High Priestess Shazeef. Please enter your
confirmation number here _____*

MacGregor looked over the message. "I figured as
much."

"Is the high priestess onto us?" asked Leyla. "Can the
police trace that phone? Why can't we make a call to New
Lydia?"

"That phone is used by the guild when we don't wish
to be discovered. It is on the network but hidden. I think it
is time to fill you in on the situation in New Lydia," said
MacGregor. "We live under tyranny. It is a tyranny of literal
interpretation of the Scriptures of the Ancient Faith, an

extremely charismatic high priestess, and a crew of highly motivated priests who support her."

"I don't understand," said Leyla. "Isn't the purpose of the Ancient Faith to help all humanity?"

Hugh MacGregor laughed a bit. It was a laugh not unlike that of the man with the flashlight. "High Priestess Shazeef believes that the Bavianer are sentient beings and should be converted to the Ancient Faith. It is through our own prejudice that humans are at war with them. She has been using a legal tool called the Right of Eminent Domain to seize property and turn it into Bavianer habitat. The policy is called Forgiveness, Relocation, and Reconciliation. The policy is highly favored by those within Santa Fe, especially in the seminary here with the students. Outside the walls of Santa Fe the policy is resented. The reason for such a policy being a continuing problem is that Shazeef never seems to lose on any matter, so she can swindle us working folks to further her ideology."

"She's wrong about the Bavianer," said Greamand. "I remember these debates within the priesthood. We haven't really been able to connect with the Bavianer. We don't feel their minds; we live in different realities. The reason we have negative views on the creatures is their behavior; it isn't our views that cause the behavior."

"Shazeef disagrees," replied MacGregor. "The most recent and pressing problem that the Shepherds Guild has with her is that she wishes to turn the Northeast Grassland in the Santa Fe District into another Bavianer forest. Such a thing will cut into the guild's interests to say the least."

"Hold on," said Murdo. "I've never heard this before, and I travel through that area all the time."

"It isn't public yet," replied MacGregor. "I have sources in her private council meetings. You need to remember that we are an important part of the economy, but we are not essential. Santa Fe's main economic activity is the seminary and its associated industries. They get funding from interested people on Earth too. Shazeef gets big-time funding from Earth people who are both inside and outside of the faith. Those outside the faith fund her because they are interested in her ideas. There are also many students from Earth who attend the seminary in this town. It warps politics here."

"Is it possible to come up with some agreement with the Bavianer?" asked Leyla. "It seems those of Aviabron have done so."

MacGregor answered, "The high priestess can make them do some tricks, but it is always touch-and-go. They're pretty dangerous. It is probably like that in Aviabron. We must shut down the grassland-to-forest idea, and to do so, we need a moral victory against the high priestess."

"What exactly would a moral victory look like?" asked Greamand.

"You must get your imprisoned comrade out of jail, and your entire team must get to New Lydia with your message," replied MacGregor. He folded his hands. Leyla noticed that his fingernails were well groomed and his hands were soft.

"Why can't we three just go from here to New Lydia for your moral victory?" asked Greamand, his voice becoming deep and suspicious.

"Then you will have only passed through, leaving a comrade on the battlefield so to speak," replied MacGregor. "We need a deliberate act of defiance. The Bavianer regularly assault the working class, attacking those who live in the outer district near their homes or those who work outside within the city limits—it's a steady drip of outrages that the government completely ignores. No amount of pleading and no amount of these outrages have changed the policy. People in power don't drop their ideology when it is threatened. They cling to it more tightly. I know that a jailbreak will make the news. After the news, there will be speculation as to why a messenger from Hattusa was thrown in prison when he was just trying to save his city. This will help change the minds of students, ambitious lower priests, businessmen, and civil servants about Shazeef and her policy. The high priestess will lose critical support, and we may have a different person in that office come the next Sacred Elections. The scandal might even bring about a revival of an independent secular government. Theocracy is dull and grim and bad for profit." MacGregor then laughed. "Prophets are bad for profits! Do you get the pun?"

"I don't think your method is what is needed right now," said Greamand. He got the pun but wasn't smiling. "If we get to New Lydia, we can use diplomatic pressure to free Harold. We can hire a lawyer and pay for bail to rescue Harold in a way that is less risky. This way, we might not get there at all."

MacGregor's face made a twitch. Before, his expressions were pleasant, or at least neutral, but now a hint of murderous rage appeared. It was unnerving to watch. Leyla felt immediate stunning fear; Greamand felt a returning anger, made sharper by his continued pain; and Murdo felt astonishment.

MacGregor continued, "I may just give the high priestess a call and tell her I have three fugitives here if you don't help out."

"You can't do that. You gave us sanctuary through the oaths of the Shepherds Guild," said Murdo.

"You know the oaths as well as I," replied MacGregor. "I am obligated to help a distressed fellow shepherd if *I find*

121

him worthy. I don't know if you are worthy or not." His face returned to a pleasant setting. "Come, let us make our plans."

Leyla looked at the other two and said, "I know I'm not really a part of Messenger Platoon Six, but you can't imagine the horrors that Harold saved me from. I will do what I can to help him out." Then, looking at MacGregor, Leyla said, "Count me in."

Chapter 10

In the Jail of High Priestess Shazeef of Santa Fe

Harold's cell was completely made from adobe brick, excepting the iron bars that made the door and the iron bars that covered a window to the outdoors. The cell held a bed, a toilet, a single wooden chair, and a sink. There was a toothbrush, towel, and bar of soap on the bed. The window let in light and air—more light outside now than when he was arrested. Messenger Platoon Six had arrived in Santa Fe during Fulldark and lingered at the hospital through Ascent. It was now getting to Fullday. Harold looked out. He could see the alleyway behind the jail. "Santa Fe is filled with alleyways," he muttered.

"What is that?" asked a gruff woman's voice.

Harold turned around, surprised to hear a voice and have a visitor. A thin, tall woman with a sunken face and very thin lips looked at him. She was dressed in the red robes of a priestess and had the white sash that indicated she was a high priestess. With a start, Harold realized that she was the high priestess of Santa Fe. Behind her were two young priests with chiseled, handsome faces and short, sandy brown hair. In front of her was a disheveled policeman with a thin mustache and a rumpled, wool tunic. The policeman was holding a ring of keys.

"You are the one who killed the Bavianer," she said.

Harold didn't answer.

"Silence, eh. Don't bother; I already know. One of my sources saw the great fire and then noticed four people on three camels. You match the description of one of the suspects. We have security camera footage and have put two and two together. Where are the others?"

"I don't know," answered Harold. "We got separated."

"How did you get separated? What are those murderers doing?" hissed High Priestess Shazeef.

"We got separated when I was arrested," said Harold.

"Don't get smart with me," said High Priestess Shazeef. "You don't even realize yet the full scope of the trouble you are in." She looked past Harold and said, "Boys, they only destroy." Looking back at Harold, she asked, "You're wearing a militia jacket with Hattusa markings. Where did you get it?"

"I am a member of the Hattusa militia on militia business," answered Harold.

The high priestess drew a large breath and said, "The Hattusa militia has no business here. This incident becomes far more serious. I know the high priestess in Hattusa. She'll have you flayed alive for being a rogue soldier."

The high priestess's eyes made a flash as she said "flayed alive." Her face and thin features had a vague, dark beauty, which age had not been able to bury. *Perhaps it's her eyes*, Harold thought. They were large, hypnotic, and even more jewellike than Leyla's. They were an emerald green—and bright. In her youth, Shazeef must have caused many a fistfight between eager suitors. Now, she had no suitors but, instead, battalions of capable men eager to follow her every whim.

This contrasted greatly with the high priestess in Hattusa. She was more a bully, a loudmouth, a hanger-on and toady of better people. The high priestess of Hattusa would never be able to flay anyone alive. She'd faint at the sight of blood. Harold thought of the heavy walking woman and figured she was in her office, drunk, only venturing out to occasionally throw incense in the fire at sacred stone circle. What comfort could such a person give to the grieving families in Hattusa? Harold almost laughed, but the situation was so very serious. He decided to own up, to say what he was doing and try and convince the high priestess to help him. "I'm not a rogue soldier, madam," replied Harold. "I'm a messenger traveling through Santa Fe to New Lydia. Hattusa is in grave danger. It is under siege from a force of Bavianer led by humans from Aviabron. Should Hattusa fall, we believe that the Mighty River will be diverted to the basin, in which Aviabron is situated. This valley, this city, these farms, all of this will become nothing more than blowing dirt if we fail."

"You're wrong, young man," answered the high priestess. "What is it that you know?"

Harold realized the question was meant to say he didn't know anything. It wasn't a question at all.

High Priestess Shazeef continued on. "Tolerance and coexistence!" she cried. "You know nothing but fighting. There is so much more. Unilateral tolerance, relocation, and reconciliation will end the constant fighting on this moon. It will usher in a new golden age of prosperity, rights, and true oneness with the gods of the Ancient Faith.

She paused again. Harold had the feeling that she was starting a sermon or a lecture that she normally gave.

Shazeef continued, "The reason there is trouble between man and the Bavianer is the fault of humanity. The central pillar of trouble is our own intolerance. The reason for the low level conflicts—the sniping, sword swinging, shooting, and ambuscades—is the attitudes that we carry on in our hearts. If you change the attitudes, you change the outcome. It is time to open up a new chapter of understanding."

Harold was about to say that his understanding of Bavianer was that they were a shrewd, violent animal, but the high priestess wasn't conversing; she was preaching.

She continued, "The Bavianer's actions are a natural reaction to our hatred toward them. With a new policy of mutual understanding, we can share this moon and grow in our Ancient Faith."

As the high priestess preached away, Harold wondered to himself how, exactly, humans and Bavianer could really come to understanding through religion. Harold immediately saw several problems with this theory. The Ancient Faith was a faith built on protest, on dissent. As such, any idea could take hold of a faction of the Ancient Faith, and that idea could split the faith in some way; or it could drive out other spiritual leaders due to fashionable moralist causes they were unsure of.

Harold remembered when, a few years ago, everyone in Hattusa had worn blue Caps of Faith. They wore blue based on a sermon preached by a traveling Priest of New Lydia who had stopped by in Hattusa. Harold didn't really remember why blue was so important, only that it had been a big deal for some of the older kids. Eventually the blue caps had gone out of fashion, but the caps could have seriously divided the faithful of Hattusa. How could the Bavianer keep up with the constantly changing social-based code of morality when Harold had a hard time doing so?

Harold also thought about Greamand. He had every official prayer in the book memorized, but he still had doubts. How could the Bavianer, who were pretty witless in most ways, hold a martyr's faith when the gods of all humanity were so silent and abstract?

Harold figured that the Illissos settlers like him were at constant odds with the creatures due to a genuine conflict of interest. The humans in Aviabron did have a sort of understanding with the creatures, but it was more a mutual pact to carry out a specific end. If, or when—Harold gulped hard, cringing in guilt at his doubt in his home—Hattusa surrendered, the Bavianer and Aviabron humans would likely take to fighting each other, as the mutual goal that held their alliance together would be gone.

Harold though about interrupting with his ideas, but the high priestess continued to speak in firm, even tones. Also, Harold had a hard time getting the words to form in his mouth. It seemed so easy to pick apart the problem in the silence of his mind—essentially the high priestess believed that her religious certainty could resolve a conflict that may well be intractable.

When thinking back upon his utter inability to speak later, he would realize the problems that had stopped him from articulating his countering vision. First, his knowledge of religious law was lacking, so he couldn't quote scripture to counter what she quoted to him. Second, his status at the moment was pretty low. When a person is dirty, tired, hungry, and under arrest, as it turns out, he will find it quite hard to handle a debate of high ideas against a powerful woman with beautiful, hypnotic eyes. Finally, deep down, Harold himself had heard the Universalist ideas in his religious classes at the Hattusa Temple of Worship, and he could see her logic to a degree. To reject the logic meant rejecting the universal absolutes of the gods of all humanity—or perhaps the gods of all humanity and all humanlike beings in all life-supporting planets.

As Harold thought these things, the priestess continued to forcefully put forward her position on the Bavianer. She was getting rid of hatred in the hearts of humans; she was giving affirmative rights to any Bavianer in the Santa Fe district; she had organized food drives to feed them; she had taken marginal farmland and created and improved-upon Bavianer habitat through importing and planting trees.

In a clear, forceful voice, High Priestess Shazeef said, "It is up to people who are strong in our Ancient Faith to lead humanity and Bavianer in reconciliation. It is unfortunate that much of the current climate of fear, rejection, and antagonism toward Bavianer is carried out by some priests of our Ancient Faith, but they are few in number and getting smaller. The truth is that a change in legal status and official policy changes hearts and minds. Here in Santa Fe, we are inclusive to Bavianer as part of the divine."

Shazeef raised her arms to the ceiling, looked up, and said, "We came to this moon due to our religious beliefs. We came here to more fully achieve the truth, which our faith so mightily proclaims. I was reading our scriptures and pondering the nature of Illissos when I realized that a good turn given to those who are different and misunderstood will change everything. We need to be helping, supporting, and loving." The high priestess then looked down. "Indeed, we must set on high the Bavianer. We must place them at the right hand of all that is good. If we do this, we save ourselves, and we save humanity, wherever they are in the universe."

Harold saw his chance to speak and said, with all the courage he could summon, "The Bavianer killed my father.

They wiped out most of our militia. I don't think that idea will work out in the long run."

High Priestess Shazeef's face went from red to purple.

"You're wrong. You'll see. My policy has made Santa Fe the safest city on the Mighty River. We don't have a Bavianer problem."

"I beg to differ, madam. You feed the Bavianer through the efforts of the outer farmers. They are the ones paying for this, and it isn't peaceful there." Harold realized that his arguments weren't persuading the high priestess, or the policemen, or the two hard-faced priests behind the priestess. One of the priests clenched his jaw and fastened his very hard, ice blue eyes on Harold. When he saw the priest clench his jaw in a fit of repressed rage, Harold felt an icy stab of fear in his heart. The priestess gestured to the policeman with the keys. He opened the door, and the three robed ministers entered the cell.

"Leave us," the high priestess said to the policeman. Her face returned to its normal color. Calm took hold of her. "Sit down, young man."

Harold sat on a wooden chair in the center of the room. He didn't know what else to do but follow instructions.

"It is a pity that you haven't seen the rest of this city," said Shazeef. "The gardens at the shopping district are made to resemble the hanging gardens of Babylon. The seminary and its campus is an oasis of green grass and superlative architectural design. Ivy vines cover much of the building and administrative offices. Young people come from across the galaxy seeking and finding higher meaning."

The high priestess stopped and looked into Harold's eyes. "Did you hear that? Illissos isn't the only place where the gods of the Ancient Faith are worshipped. We get funding from all sorts of places. At Hattusa, you frontier folk are so cut off. We here can get what we want, when we want it—as long as it is scripturally correct of course. Yes, many in the settler colonies on the planets Freya, Titan, and Gaia follow our teachings. The industrial areas on Earth, in the big North English mill towns, also send us students. From Earth, they go to the New Mexico spaceport, zip from there to New Lydia, and then take the train here. The other planets have their own spaceport, but the students all arrive on our wonderful train. We have special tours of the Bavianer forests, where the students can learn about the peaceful Bavianer and their wonderful ways, so harmonious with nature. Who needs local farmers and their irrigation problems here? My ministry is a river of bounty to this city. The only thing the secular city government does here is organize garbage collection."

Harold didn't know what to say to this, but he knew that he couldn't let the high priestess stop his mission. There might not be another home for him if Hattusa surrendered and was destroyed. If life got too hard on Illissos, he *could* flee, but that was an uncertain proposition. Religious repression could return on Earth or any other planet his family could flee to, and he didn't really want to leave the Ancient Faith for a new religion he might not understand or even begin to believe. He was stuck in the conflict of the here and now.

"I think you're wrong," answered Harold uncertainly. "The Bavianer won't take to the Ancient Faith, and there is no possibility for them to become civilized to our level. They are surrounding my family and everyone I know, and they mean to kill them. We need help. What happens when they choose you as their enemies, high priestess?"

Smack! A fist of one of the priests caught Harold unaware, and he was knocked out of his chair onto the ground. Harold saw a flash of light, and then he felt the swelling under his eye. Both of the priests grabbed Harold and put him back on the chair. *It came from the left*, Harold thought.

"As we have a deeper walk with the gods of all humanity, it is up to us to always take the high road." The high priestess said this in a way that was almost a song.

The strong arms of the two priests got Harold back on the wooden chair. Harold couldn't help but crouch away from the priest on his left.

When he tried to stand up, he was pushed back down by a very strong hand. Even if he stood, there wasn't much he could do. The iron bars were locked, and not only where the priests much bigger and stronger, should he be able to overwhelm them and move against the high priestess, she'd summon the police. He was trapped.

He decided that words were his best weapon. "What if there is no high road? What if we must simply fight for our own? What if justice might not ever come? I'm not sure your ideas count as justice when we in Hattusa are under this constant threat from the Bavianer."

The high priestess smiled; it was a smile that was sharklike and cruel. Her eyes still held a hard-edged, angry look. "Were you traveling with an ex-priest?"

Harold didn't answer. He tried to keep a straight face, but he realized that his expression must have been an astonished affirmation when the high priestess clapped her hands together once.

"Ha!" She gave a single laugh and looked up toward the ceiling. "I knew it. The security camera footage looked just like him. He was hunched over on that camel. I hope he is in great pain."

Harold was less than surprised that the high priestess was so glad to see someone she didn't like hurting. The woman exuded a cruel charisma. It was the sort of charisma that could rally her faithful followers against any enemy, but it was unsettling to see this charisma used against someone Harold had come to care for.

"Did he take a nice interest in you?" asked the high priestess.

"I don't understand what you mean," answered Harold. It was clear now to Harold that High Priestess Shazeef knew whom he was traveling with. It was also clear she was greatly interested in Greamand.

"Playing naive, are you?" replied Shazeef. "Do you know how he got that scar?"

"No," replied Harold.

"A young seminary student slashed him with a razor. Greamand tried to take some unnatural liberties. The scandal shook the entire priesthood in New Lydia. The Secular Authority ordered his banishment after a council of priests demanded it. Do you know what the worst of all he did was?"

Harold didn't answer. Instead, he shook his head no.

"He was unsure of the certain absolutes of the Ancient Faith. He was unsure that it could save all sentient beings, he was unsure that there was even a point of converting those not already born into the faith. He has the strange idea that the purpose of religion is to serve humanity, not the other way around. What purpose of humankind is there except to serve the glory of the gods of all humanity?"

"It seems that *things*, like religion, serving humanity, rather than humanity serving things is an idea worth looking at," answered Harold.

High Priestess Shazeef turned a dark color, her face set upon a cruel expression, and she hissed, "It is your own attitude that brought the Bavianer against you in Hattusa. It is your own guilty soul. The Bavianer are sentient beings that need our message."

This statement made Harold pretty mad, and he answered sharply, "That isn't true. The Bavianer are used by Aviabron humans so that they can dam the river and divert the water."

Smack! From the right this time, Harold was knocked on the floor. He didn't get up. Instead, he looked at the high priestess and said, "I am not a criminal. I'm a messenger under orders and in uniform to deliver a message. You are torturing an official delegate from Hattusa."

"*Enough of this*," High Priestess Shazeef shouted. "Don't expect to get out of here for a long time. You have no diplomatic immunity. You are just a crook and a murderer. Your unenlightened religious views won't turn my Santa Fe into a reactionary haven."

Then the kicks started to come. One bash hit his face. Harold didn't feel pain so much as a hard push, and then there was another. Then it was lights out. Harold's last conscious thought was that the boot on the priest's' foot needed polish.

When he regained consciousness, Harold was alone in the prison. He felt his face; it was caked in dried blood, his left eye was swollen, and his lips were bloody. He walked to the door. "Help," he croaked. "Jailer, I need medical attention."

The echo in the jailhouse indicated that he was in an empty wing of the police station. He was alone. He tried the door—locked. He washed his face in the sink and sat down on the bed. The hard, wooden chair was too horrible a machine now to sit on.

Exhaustion.

There was no other way to put it. He wanted sleep. Harold had a vague notion that he should try and stay awake if he had a concussion. His head, the area around the brain, didn't hurt, but his face did. He did a quick times table … the sevens. He'd always found that hard to remember in grammar school, but now the numbers came to him easily. He possibly had no brain injury, so with nothing else to do, Harold sank under the waves of sleep.

Harold dreamed the torture again—the crashing fists, the kicking boots, the laughing high priestess.

Then Harold's dream shifted. There was a voice; Harold couldn't tell who was the speaker was or where the voice came from. First, it reminded Harold he had wanted a sword quite badly to kill a Bavianer to prove he was a man and able to take on adult responsibilities. "Do you like adulthood now?" the voice asked sarcastically.

Then Harold discovered he was in a courtroom with a jury box. The courtroom, the chairs, the walls, the jury box, and the judge's seat were painted completely white. The jury box was filled with dark black and brown Bavianer, who snarled at him and then tore the seats of the jury box to shreds. The Bavianer then snarled at Harold again. One of the creatures, a buck with silver paws, said "Guilty" in a loud, gravelly voice. It was impossible for a Bavianer to speak, but this was just a dream, and dreams carry along in their own nonsensical but meaningful way.

In the dream, Harold turned his back on the creatures and walked toward the blank space where he presumed the door away from the white room would be, away from judgment by his enemies. He awoke after not finding the door, his dream-self's hands frantically feeling the white wall for an exit.

There is nothing like a beating to make a person think. When Harold woke up, he kept thinking about what the high priestess had said. Was Harold guilty of some deep inner hatred that had caused the Bavianer siege? Was the whole thing a misunderstanding? Were his mission and all this sacrifice not worth it?

Harold tried to open the jail door; it was locked. He tried to see if he could twist the iron bars in the window—too hard. He tried to see if the adobe bricks were soft enough to scrape through, but they were very hard. It seemed, for now, that Harold was stuck. He decided to try and make a break for it when the next feeding time came. Harold began to plan.

***

Leyla, on the other hand was beginning to really dislike Hugh MacGregor. It wasn't because he was in incapable sort of man. In fact, just the opposite was true—MacGregor was very intelligent but only in a singular way. MacGregor understood the sheep business through and through. He could discuss the importance of cobalt deficiency in the soil and how that affected sheep, and he discussed carding, felting, weaving, industrial looms, and wool production. He went on and on about the best recipes for mutton and lamb chops. After the revolution, according to MacGregor, the big issue was dung beetles. Insect life on Illissos had evolved differently from that on earth, and MacGregor wanted to import dung beetles to help manage the sheep droppings in the district and improve the soil. All through this tedium, MacGregor gave Leyla long, hungry looks. The men who'd captured her had made the same look, and that had led to …

But that was in the past; she was going to focus on freeing Harold. The news shows on TV were reporting that a dangerous ex-priest was loose in Santa Fe. Photos of Greamand were on every comms device, and wanted posters were springing up all over town with his description. MacGregor's plan was to provide Leyla with a horse and explosives to free Harold from the jail, and Harold and Leyla would travel on a fast horse to the train station. Greamand would be hidden in a barrel on a cart driven by Murdo and MacGregor, and the four would get on the train to New Lydia at the last minute. The plan seemed simple enough. Critical was that the train was not under the jurisdiction of Santa Fe. Once on it, one might have been in New Lydia.

Leyla was given a shaped charge from MacGregor and was shown pictures of where to place the bomb that would blow a hole in the outer wall, which would in turn free Harold. When she asked MacGregor where the bomb had come from and how he knew this particular stretch of wall was the right one, MacGregor answered with a simple word—"Sources"—and he would say no more. When she asked why MacGregor needed them for a moral victory against the high priestess and why MacGregor wouldn't plant bombs himself, MacGregor didn't bother to respond, he just leered at her with that hungry look.

***

Harold was alone in his cell. He was sharpening the end of a plastic toothbrush to use as a weapon during his escape when Leyla's voice called to him through the bars. At first he thought he was dreaming or hearing things, but he stood up, looked through the window, and saw Leyla. It was the most wonderful thing to look into her kind eyes, especially in that place. He was too overwhelmed with emotion to speak.

Leyla didn't miss a beat. "Quick," she said, "get away from the wall and cover yourself with the mattress." It was the sweetest voice Harold had ever heard.

Harold picked up the mattress, backed as far from the outside wall as possible, and ducked under the mattress like it was a shield. Despite the precaution, Harold was knocked back by the pressure from an explosion. It felt as though the air had turned to hardened steel for a second; the pressure stabbed at his ears, creating an enormous but brief pain. It ended with a ringing in his ears that covered over any other sound.

When he looked at the outer wall, there was a hole large enough to escape through. He dashed for it. Harold felt something wet on his face; he was bleeding from his nose. Immediately, a siren sounded from the police station. To Harold's front, Leyla sat on a gray horse. She was in clean clothes and looked wonderful. Her hair had been brushed and was sleek. He climbed onto the horse behind her, and they were off.

"Where did you get a bomb? And where did you get this horse?" asked Harold.

"No time for questions; just hang on. The police are after us," replied Leyla.

Harold could smell Leyla's perfume; it was lilac. It was the most wonderful smell, contrasting wonderfully with stale air of the prison.

Suddenly there was a noise—a cross between a *zip* and a *cra-a-a-a-k*. "Bullets!" shouted Harold. He looked back.

Three policemen were on the street a hundred feet behind them. One of the policemen was the tall, broad-shouldered bald man who had done the paperwork on Harold. He was in the center of the street, standing erect and watching the fleeing pair with a wry smile. A policeman on the left was buttoning his blue tunic—the escape had apparently caught him unaware, and he was frantically getting his uniform right. On the right, there was a man who had taken a knee and was aiming a black rifle at Harold and Leyla.

"They're aiming at us Leyla. We need to get off the street," said Harold.

Leyla replied in a mischievous tone, "Just hang on." She took a hard right turn toward the right side of the street and then bobbed again to the left. The horse was quite agile, and if Harold hadn't had so much riding experience growing up, he'd have been knocked off the horse. But he held on, gripping with his knees.

When they reached the intersection, Leyla directed the horse left. She was in the center of town, where the stables were located, and suddenly a man opened a gate and a flock of hundreds and hundreds of sheep were released onto the street behind them. There were bleats and cries and running animals everywhere. Harold vowed he would eternally be indebted to all sheep and shepherds, in gratitude for the blessed accident.

With that thought, Harold realized that Murdo had something to do with the escaping animals. While passing the stables, he craned his neck to see if he could see Clem and the other camels, but they were out of sight. *How will I get my camels back?* Harold put the thought out of his mind. He needed to focus on escape.

The horse thundered down the street. To his right, Harold noticed a sacred stone circle, a normal public symbol of the Ancient Faith. What was strange about this was, at the center, was a figure, made of wax or papier-mâché—Harold couldn't really tell. The figure was that of a wounded Bavianer; its arms were stretched to the sky in the same way that the priests stretched their arms at the end of a religious event.

It was an image every bit as unsettling as the TV program with the folkie singer and dancing Bavianer. In this case, the high priestess had put the Bavianer idol—there was no other word to refer to the wax figure—in the spot the voice of the ancient gods of all humanity was said to occupy during religious ceremonies "where two or more were gathered in their name."

The imagery had a clear meaning; the downtrodden and oppressed Bavianer were like gods in some way. The Ancient Faith cultivated in its followers a deep sense of internal, individual guilt, while at the same time cultivating a yearning for perfection against sin in society in general and in the individual in particular. The problem was that the Great Dissenter had many passages in his scriptures about sin and how to find perfection against sin, but these scriptures could be interpreted in a variety of ways. These passages were often strongly interpreted in one light by some faction while, at the same time, some social condition or social vice could be raised to the level of high sin or high sainthood based on the mood and organizational skill of the various priests and laymen. In Santa Fe, Harold realized that the Bavianer problem had been sanctified. Santa Fe was engaged in a sort of Bavianer worship, where they kept as far from the Bavianer as possible in real life, but made them dancing pets in TV shows, objects of pity in sermons, and subjects of largess in tax policy. The costs were paid for by the working people of Santa Fe but not the well-connected power players in the city, especially at the seminary.

Greamand was right. In Santa Fe, the Ancient Faith was an entirely different thing than it was in Hattusa. No wonder Messenger Platoon Six was having so much trouble in Santa

Fe. This also helped clarify why Greamand wanted to go to New Lydia in person and why he'd wanted to skip Santa Fe entirely. In New Lydia, Greamand had to make sure he spoke to the right people, the people who were not under the spell of Shazeef and her religious concepts.

A few turns at a solid gallop, and Harold saw the train station. A sign with a clock ticked down the seconds until the train left the station. There was less than a minute left.

The train itself was bright chrome. The windows were not regular rectangles but cut in a rounded, sleek way, giving the impression that the train was fast even when sitting at the station. Because of the light from Boreas and the Fullday sun, the train's iridescent chrome skin flashed different colors in an instant. First there was Boreas Blue and then violet and then green and finally red. Harold had never seen such a flashy sight. It contrasted with the adobe that made up so much of the Illissos settlements.

"We must get on the train," said Leyla. "We'll be home free then." They got off the horse and started for the passenger door on the gleaming train.

Just then, a shout rang out. "Halt."

Harold turned. There was a policeman, and the badge on his blue fez reflected the sunlight into Harold's eyes. The policeman was holding the hollow tube. Suddenly, Lela was gripped in the same electric paralysis that had seized Harold earlier. Harold looked around. A well-dressed man in a smoker's jacket and black felt pants surveyed the scene with an air of detachment. When he looked over at Leyla, his face changed to the expression of eager want. Harold decided that whatever happened next, he wouldn't leave Leyla. He'd make a stand.

Chapter 11

Danger on the Train

It all happened so fast. Leyla was still laid out on the ground and twitching from the policeman's electric blast. Both Harold and Leyla were only several feet from the train's passenger door. From that door came Murdo. He yelled out a noise that sounded something like *arrrrrgggh*, but with a harshness that, to Harold, seemed to convey exhaustion in the *gggh* parts of the scream. While he screamed, Murdo threw something at the policeman. It was a smoke grenade, taken, Harold would later discover, from the stores of the Shepherds Guild. The air filled with a thick bright green smoke that smelled horribly. Harold reached down and grabbed Leyla. She was just beginning to come around again, and together, they boarded the train. Murdo guided them to a private compartment, where Greamand was waiting. Greamand's face was white, and he was clearly in pain.

On schedule and oblivious to the furious struggle at the station, the train's operator pulled the train away from the station. Harold watched the scene from the window outside. The green smoke filled the station, but the wind whipped it in different directions, providing Harold occasional glimpses of the policeman calling on his radio.

"We're safe now," said Murdo. "The train is under the jurisdiction of New Lydia. We won't be bothered here."

Murdo and Leyla then explained all that had happened while Harold was in jail.

"Greamand," said Harold, "you're right. The high priestess in New Lydia has a totally different view on how the Ancient Faith applies to the Bavianer conflict. She preaches a sort of tolerance, but while she preached to me, her priests beat me unconscious."

"We were fortunate you were awake when I came to rescue you," said Leyla. "The entire escape operation was based on perfect timing. We really lucked out."

There was excitement all around that the plan had worked.

"I need to have a word with the conductor," said Greamand. "I wish to cable Sadra, the high priest of New Lydia and tell him the situation. Our mission is now in the truly critical phase. I need to gather my allies in New Lydia before we deliver my message."

The compartment in which the travelers found themselves was made of wooden paneling. The trim on the wooden paneling was the same bright chrome that the train's outer skin had been constructed of. The compartment's seats where made of leather and filled with a plush stuffing. There were windows, through which Harold could see into the aisle of the passenger car. It was empty. On the wall was a touch screen console. Greamand pushed an icon on the glowing screen that showed a picture of a conductor.

"Greamand," said Harold, "High Priestess Shazeef said that the reason for the conflict was human attitudes. Is this true?"

"Possibly," replied Greamand, "but the attitudes of us Illissos settlers are partially formed by the actions the

Bavianer take. Of course, our being in close proximity to the Bavianer is what causes the problems to arise. However, it is not possible to find a lasting peace, when one side of a conflict believes that the answer is a religious idealism that the other side cannot fully comprehend. This especially won't work when the other side is actively pursuing hostilities."

Greamand made another jump.

"I have some painkillers in the supply bag," said Murdo. "Would you like them now?"

"Not yet, maybe not ever," said Greamand. "I want to deliver the cable to High Priest Sadra. I need my mind sharp. Those painkillers from the Shepherds Guild stores are pretty medically suspect. It might even be poison. All those supplies are illicit. They are illegal payment for our part in Hugh MacGregor's commercial, money-chasing revolution. I don't want any more part of that revolution, and I want a clear head for what is to come."

The conductor arrived. He was carrying a comms device that was more like a clipboard. Greamand stood and met him outside the passenger compartment. Harold watched Greamand speak to the conductor through the windows of the passenger compartment. The conductor was a relaxed-looking man. He wore a blue suit that was not unlike the suit of the Santa Fe police forces, except it was a deeper shade of blue and there was a decorative cord on the conductor's tunic. The two men talked, the conductor made some entries on the electronic clipboard, and Greamand gave the conductor several coins.

"That is done," said Greamand as he returned. "Now for rest until we get to New Lydia. Sadra will meet us at the station. He won't let me down."

Outside, it was still light, but it was waning light. Descent would start soon.

"What other things do you have in that bag?" asked Harold. He was pointing to a green backpack Murdo was carrying.

Murdo answered, "I had, and used one smoke grenade. I have a change of clothes for you and this stunner." Murdo pulled out a hollow tube, like the one used by the Santa Fe police. "It is a bit weaker than the police model, though."

"What about our rifles?" asked Harold.

"They're still in Santa Fe," answered Murdo. "Couldn't be helped leaving them there. We had to be inconspicuous in Santa Fe, and Greamand hid in the Shepherds Guild building until we transported him in a barrel to the station."

"You know," replied Harold, "that the high priestess had sensors all through the Bavianer forest. I wonder why she didn't have any in the city that could have detected us."

"That could be the reason," answered Leyla. "She had all the sensors in the forest; there was nothing left over in the city."

"Ha," said Greamand. "She squandered her resources on protecting the wrong thing. Now MacGregor has won his moral victory."

"You mean *we* won his moral victory," answered Leyla. "That man is a fraud. He used us to further his aims without taking any risks personally. At any rate, Harold, we have clean clothes for you."

Leyla pulled off Harold's jacket. Harold was ashamed of himself. The jacket reeked terribly, but Leyla didn't say anything. She must have smelled the terrible odor coming off of his jacket. It was a smell that mixed sweat, camel, jail, dirt, manure, and smoke together. She pulled from Murdo's supply bag a pile of shepherd's clothing not unlike what Murdo and Greamand were wearing. "Hang on," said Harold. "I can change in private."

Harold went to the lavatory. It was located on the far end of a different car. Harold left his car and went across the passageway that led to the lavatory. On the way he passed a happy group of train riders. Nobody seemed to recognize the fact that Harold had been a wanted man in Santa Fe. The travelers were also incurious as to why the train had pulled away from the station while the station was filled with policemen and green, smoking clouds. The passengers were all busy with their own lives. There were giggles and flirtations between the men and women. Some people merely looked into their comms devices. The majority of his fellow passengers looked a bit older than Harold but still very young. Perhaps they were students for the seminary. One of the young women had a shirt with a printing on it. Harold had never seen such a thing before in Hattusa, where so many of the clothes were homespun. The shirt's printing had big letters that read, "DEEPEN YOUR WALK WITH THE GODS OF ALL HUMANITY," and below that, in smaller print, "Santa Fe of Illissos."

Once in the lavatory, Harold washed up and returned to the compartment in clean clothes. He sat down next to Leyla and fell fast asleep.

***

A jolt woke Harold. All the others were also sleeping in the compartment. Leyla looked like an angel, and Murdo was sleeping with a frown on his face. Greamand looked as though he'd lost twenty pounds. Lines of pain etched his face; the Bavianer wounds on his arms were clearly hurting him.

It was to be a long train ride from Santa Fe to New Lydia—easier, of course, than walking or going by camel, but they were stuck on the train. The police in Santa Fe knew they were on the train, and they could very well have radioed ahead for someone to stop them when they got off at the station in New Lydia. Harold imagined a knife-wielding assassin but then relaxed when he remembered that Santa Fe and New Lydia didn't cooperate so much on political matters, and a political arrest in Santa Fe would not be recognized in New Lydia. It was very likely the two cities only cooperated to keep the trains safely running on time.

Fullday was over, and Descent was well on. Harold looked out the window at the scenery outside. The blue twilight was overtaking the final rays of sunlight. Here, instead of desert, the ground was covered in pasture grass. Harold looked at a herd of bison chomping contentedly on the grass. Mixed with the bison were yaks. Both creatures had been imported from Earth but for different reasons. The bison were a great source of meat, and they could hold off Bavianer very well by themselves. The yaks were imported especially for their long fur, which could be used for fiber, yarn making, and felt making. Harold had heard that the hills around New Lydia held many of the creatures, but until now, he'd never seen one in person. The yaks thrived in the mountains, but as of yet, they hadn't been moved to Hattusa. As the train continued, the creatures fell from his vision.

Harold couldn't go back to sleep. That jolt had felt quite strange. He looked again at the window. The train was moving but not quickly, instead, the train was picking up speed. Had the train stopped? How deeply had he been sleeping? And for how long? Deeply enough to not notice the train had stopped?

For a brief moment, Harold thought that, perhaps, they'd had a scheduled stop. But there was nothing, nothing man-made, that is, out there. No, the train was supposed to go straight from Santa Fe to New Lydia. He thought it was supposed to at least, but he didn't really know. He'd lived in Hattusa all his life, and now that he was away from his farmhouse and family, the world seemed so much bigger and more complex. Off the farm, and away from the rigid schedules of school, uncertainties were everywhere. While Harold thought about this, he found that he needed to use the lavatory again.

He walked from the compartment where his companions were sleeping through the passageway between the cars to the car with the lavatory.

Harold entered the car with the lavatory expecting to see happy students, but it was empty. However, bags, books, and other carry-on items were scattered all over the car. It was as though the students had left in a hurry. Immediately the pressure on Harold's bladder went away. A sense of danger electrified Harold's blood. In the time since he had left Hattusa, Harold's instincts had sharpened to a fine edge. The situation on the train was now dangerous. Had the students been taken off the train? Was that the reason for the stop? If only he'd stayed awake.

At the end of this car was another door, which led to another car. Harold walked toward it, passed the space between the cars, and entered a storage car. In it, suitcases and boxes were stacked behind a locked metal grating. This car was used for passengers' large baggage, but Harold was free to pass through the aisle way between the cages. Beyond the car was a door, which opened to the passageway between cars. He slowly opened the door. The passageway was lit by light coming through a door window from the next car, and Harold stopped short. Through the door, he could see what was going on in the next car. The car itself was a sort of dining car; there was a bar and tables, and all the students were packed into it. The students had facial expressions ranging from blank and expressionless to keenly worried. None of the students smiled.

Two armed men stood in the midst of the group. They each held advanced rifles. They weren't the clunky wood and steel jobs that Harold and the others had been issued, and they were far more advanced than the militia carbines. These rifles were black, angular, and light. They each held a large magazine, and Harold could see they had advanced optics for the Illissos light conditions. The men were wearing roundish, black helmets and olive drab uniforms. These men weren't the light-haired people of the Ancient Faith. They looked foreign, dark, and strange. One man's face had features that resembled those of the man who'd tried to open the gate in Hattusa. The other man's face looked like a hawk, hungry and proud.

They were men from Aviabron.

Harold realized they must have camped out between Santa Fe and New Lydia, waiting to pick off any messengers. They'd used some ruse to stop the train and then hop on. One of the men was appearing to instruct the students. He laughed and smiled. He must have been saying something relaxing because the faces of the students picked up happier expressions. Harold couldn't hear what he'd said due to the noise from the train. Harold was also hidden in partial darkness. Even if someone from the well-lit dining car looked directly at Harold through the window, they wouldn't see him through the window into the darkness of the passageway.

Harold backed off. The armed men were coming for Messenger Platoon Six. The soldiers had moved the students to protect them from any cross fire. They had probably scoped the entire train and knew that Messenger Platoon

Six was sleeping in a first-class compartment. He turned and ran through the railway cars to the compartment where the others were.

"Murdo wake up," said Harold.

"What is it?" asked Murdo.

"Armed men," replied Harold. "There are at least two of them. They are three cars down."

"What!" exclaimed Leyla. "Oh, I thought we were home free."

Greamand spoke up, "Everyone, we need to relocate. Keep the reading light on in this compartment. Make this place seem full. Murdo, hang your jacket on the window. It will make it that much more difficult to see who is in the compartment."

As Murdo started to arrange the passenger compartment Leyla asked, "How will that save us?"

"They are headed for us and mean to shoot," answered Greamand. "We are going to give them an empty target, anything to make things hard for them."

"Murdo," said Harold, "the stunner. Hand it to me." Harold looked at the device. It was just a hollow plastic tube. There was no button or control on it. "How does it work?" he asked Murdo.

"You point it and rub your thumb across the spine," answered Murdo. "Remember, you've only got about three shots, perhaps four, until it needs to be charged again, so shoot wisely. When it is out of shots, the spine will turn red." Murdo said this while hanging his jacket on the window.

"Which end do I point toward the enemy?" asked Harold.

"Either end," answered Murdo. "The device won't stun the person who is holding it. Its range can cover the length of this railway car." Murdo's face wrinkled, and he added, "Most of the length of the car."

"Everyone forward," said Greamand. "We just need to hold them off for a few minutes. We have to be close to New Lydia now." He looked at the window and continued, "Yes, see the mountains. They look right. Armed gunmen from Aviabron will not be welcome in New Lydia. They probably plan to murder us and get away before the train get to the city."

The foursome started to move toward the front of the train. The swaying of the train as it made its way across the tracks made walking quickly difficult. "Wait," said Leyla "the lights." She threw a switch and the lights in the aisleway went out. The railway car they were fleeing from became shrouded in a mix of light, twilight, and darkness that was dazzling to the eye. The compartment the messengers had left appeared occupied. A close careful look at the compartment would end the ruse, but it was just enough to, perhaps, buy the messengers precious seconds.

"Good work," said Greamand. They continued to the next car. This car was filled with crates. They were tied down to grommets in the floor, but there was, again, an aisleway leading to the next car.

"Shouldn't we call the conductor?" asked Leyla.

"He might not be on our side," answered Murdo. "He must have ordered the train to stop to pick up the gunmen."

"Murdo is right," answered Greamand. "We don't know what he will do. Best let him not know we have moved."

"Go forward and check the door," whispered Harold to Murdo.

The shepherd did so.

"Locked," said Murdo. "It must lead to the conductor's car and the engine."

"Unfasten the straps and move those two boxes toward the door. We can use them as a barricade," said Greamand.

He was pointing to a group of long boxes that appeared to be good candidates for the purpose at hand.

"Then they can climb on the roof of the train and shoot down on us," said Murdo.

"Wait," said Harold. "I think that I can get the drop on them."

Without waiting for a reply, Harold moved back toward the compartment car. It was still empty and dark, except for the light in Messenger Platoon Six's former compartment. Harold was happy to see that the jacket in the window was doing a stellar job.

Then Harold saw them. The two gunmen were coming through the lighted passageway between the railway cars. Harold jumped into his car's other darkened compartment.

"Now," said a voice. It was deep, masculine, and completely relaxed, and it was followed by a terrible rip from the two men's rifles. Harold hugged the floor of the darkened compartment as the bullets tore through the place he and the others had occupied only moments earlier. Had he not awoken, they'd be dead now.

Then silence.

The two gunmen had poured all their ammunition into the compartment. Harold made his move. While remaining crouched, he opened his compartment's door, pointed the hollow tube at the first gunman and rubbed his thumb on the spine of the hollow tube stunner. The tube made a slight vibration, and the first gunman fell with a shout. Harold repeated what he'd done with the stunner, and the second gunman fell. Harold rushed toward them while they were paralyzed. He grabbed the rifle of the closest man by the barrel. Instantly, his hand was burned. The barrel was terribly hot. The rifle scattered across the aisle as Harold instinctively hurled it away. He grabbed the second rifle, this time not by the barrel. He'd disarmed the gunmen.

As he turned to pick up the rifle that had burned him, one of the men grabbed his ankle. It was a crushing grip. Harold twisted around and gave each man a second zap from the stunner. He picked up the fallen rifle, by the pistol grip this time, and ran toward the door that led to the others.

"I disarmed them," Harold said with a dry mouth.

"Lock the door," said Greamand.

Murdo turned to lock the door that led to the railway car Harold had just come from. "It doesn't lock," Murdo shouted.

"Hold the door," shouted Leyla.

Harold looked at the spine along the stunner. It hadn't turned red even though he used more than three shots. "I've likely got one more shot with the stunner," said Harold. "I'll stun the first man, and we'll clobber the second."

"No," said Murdo. "Too risky. Let's hold them off with the barricade until we get into New Lydia.

He moved a box. It was one of the crates that Greamand had pointed out earlier. The box was heavy and solid, and they positioned it to block the door. Because the railway doors between the cars slid inward to open and had glass windows, the box was the only thing that could possibly hold the two men at bay. Harold and Murdo pushed the box against the door. It covered the door but only with an inch on each side of the doorjamb. From the other side there was the sound of a sliding door opening and then a shout, and Harold could feel the two men push back against the box they were pressing against the door.

"Use the rifles," shouted Leyla. "Shoot them through the box." She had picked up a rifle and handed another one to Greamand.

"There are no bullets," explained Harold. "I couldn't stun them until they'd emptied their magazines."

The train was slowing down. It made several turns. The forward door, the one that had been locked, opened. It was the conductor. He looked at the scene and said, "What is going on?"

Greamand explained, and the conductor said, "I knew they were trouble, but the railway signal was lit for an emergency pickup. I'll summon the police to meet us at the station." He turned and ran back to where he'd come from.

"I can't hold them," said Murdo.

"Hang on," said Harold.

Then a horrible beating started on the box. The gunmen were going to ram their way in. Harold could feel the jolts sting his hands.

Outside, the blue gloom of Illissos was replaced by harsh, orange-colored, artificial light. They were coming into New Lydia at last, with the enemy, quite literally, at the gate.

Chapter 12

NEW LYDIA AT LAST

The train slowed to a crawl. They were pulling into the station at New Lydia. The conductor returned and said in a frightened but still firm tone, "Hold them just a little longer. The police will get them at the station."

Harold and Murdo strained against the repeating blows from the two gunmen. Just as Harold's arms were about to give out—silence.

The train was stopped now. Policemen burst into the car through an outer door. Harold couldn't help but feel a great mistrust toward the policemen, even as they swooped in to rescue him and the others. Here in New Lydia, the police didn't wear fezzes. Instead, they wore round, cloth hats with leather brims. The badge on the caps was a dragon holding a disk that represented Boreas.

"Yeah, we got 'em," said one of the policemen.

There were squawks and comments on the police radios, but Harold couldn't understand what was said on the devices.

The conductor helped Greamand out, and the others followed them. The conductor then moved on, saying something about, "the students' safety."

Harold looked around the station platform. The two gunmen were being led away in handcuffs, and despite being led into captivity, they walked upright, with pride. The station itself was entirely indoors and well-lit, with an abundance of electrical light. Upon the walls were frescos and mosaics showing religious stories from the faith of Illissos. Everywhere were hurried people wearing Earth-tone felt clothes. Harold was struck by just how nice the clothes were. Many of the coats didn't seem to be of the practical kind worn by Hattusa farmers but instead were cut into fashionable shapes. Many of the people wore ruffled lace on their collars and cuffs.

Leyla couldn't help but marvel at the dresses of the women. She grabbed Harold's arm and said, "Oh, look at that dress."

"Prosperity brings out the best in clothes, though not always the best in people," said Greamand.

"Don't be such a kill-joy," replied Leyla. "It is nice to see and wear pretty clothes."

Harold was still too shaken by the events on the train to get too concerned over the dresses, but he didn't mind Leyla grabbing his arm. It helped his mind become a bit steadier. The bright lights, the massive train station, and the throngs of people were overwhelming Harold, and he was glad to get the support to focus.

They walked toward the enormous arch that led out of the station to the city itself. Coming the other way, from the arch, was a collection of five priests in bright red robes. The priests traveled in a formation, like how the dots are arranged on a dice's "five" face. In the center was the high priest. He was a short man with a potbelly. His face was careworn. His hair was long, the color of silver. He looked younger than Greamand. The priests around him were tall and lean. One of the priests, the one walking behind and to the left of the high priest, had ice-blue eyes and a hard, chiseled face that reminded Harold of the priests who'd tortured him in the Santa Fe jail.

Messenger Platoon Six, led by Greamand, made its way toward the collection of priests. When the wary band closed in on the priests, Greamand stopped everyone and reached his hand out to the high priest in the center. "Sadra, my old friend ..."

Sadra, the high priest, quickly shook Greamand's hand but offered no introductions. "There is no time for chitchat, my lost brother," Sadra said while looking squarely at Greamand. "We need to get you to the Secular Authority. Chairman Somerset has called a meeting of the Privy Council. I took your message you sent from the train to the chairman right away. We knew that Hattusa had sent the militia out due to the Bavianer attack but then heard nothing—which is very strange in such a case. The Bavianer swarm is normal; no communications for so long is not."

"Sir," said Harold to High Priest Sadra, "you know that Hattusa needs help. Why can't you order the Zeppelins with armed men to help out right now?"

"The constitutional arrangements in New Lydia between the church and state are different than in Santa Fe. It's a bit more like Hattusa here, except the priests of the Ancient Faith have less power than in Hattusa. Here, we religious authorities have a different view of our place in government. We New Lydian priests focus on the soul of the individual human, not the soul of government policy. We can't order a military strike. In Santa Fe, it is a bit different. Here in New Lydia, we also run a university and seminary, but we focus on Illissos issues and Illissos students. The number of off-world students is pretty low."

The buildings and other features of New Lydia were dazzling to Harold. There were large, comfortable town houses and artificial electric lights. Most impressive was that there was very little adobe brick. The building material was sleek concrete and cut stone.

Sadra noticed that Harold was marveling at the city, and so he said, "Here, the economy of New Lydia is more advanced than those of all the other cities of the Ancient Faith, mainly because of our location at the mouth of the Mighty River and the spaceport and the mineral trade."

"And the fact that it's an older, established settlement with the nicest climate on this moon," added Greamand. He then continued, "Harold, the Secular Authority has power here, not the priests."

"How do you manage moral affairs," asked Harold, "like what the scriptures discuss?"

Sadra answered, "We do manage them, but moral issues are always hard to keep a firm grasp on. We really keep things down to a dull roar. Get married; stay married; and early to bed, early to rise are often the best you can get out of people. What we have here are the descendants of the original pioneers, who mainly police their own moral affairs. It is very likely those original pioneers were already policing their moral affairs prior to the Great Dissenter, but I digress. The Secular Authority grew out of a committee that managed land disputes and a committee that managed the militia. It grew to be a stable government with a functioning Register of Deeds Office. This is a marvelous accomplishment. Once you get that, don't let it go. How the secular and religious authorities separated into different branches is a historical topic of infinite interest to me. I'm writing a book on the subject."

"Sadra," said Greamand, "how quickly do you think we can get a military operation to relieve Hattusa?"

Sadra sighed and then said, "I think there will be some hesitation, but in the end, the New Lydian military will intervene."

"But will you intervene soon enough to save Hattusa?" asked Harold.

Sadra looked at Harold and said, "I am not here to fail. I'm going to lend all my weight to get the Secular Authority to intervene. While the priests of the Ancient Faith and the Secular Authority are separate constitutional authorities, we can work together to do what is right." Sadra continued, "It is important to know that Chairman Somerset understands the situation, the big picture at least, and many of his advisors have been warning about the Aviabron settlement and its people for some time."

"I thought that there was missionary work to the place," said Murdo, "at least from Santa Fe."

Sadra answered, "There is missionary work from New Lydia also. However, many of the missionaries are returning to New Lydia uncertain that they are going to be able to convert anyone there."

"That's a big admission," replied Greamand. "When I was a young man, before the plague, nearly every priest insisted that the whole of humanity would be converted to the Ancient Faith from the Illissos springboard."

"I'm not as old as you," replied Sadra, "but I do remember reading about those ideas. Mind you, it isn't most missionaries who are drawing such conclusions. It's only the ones who've come away from Aviabron who are more wary. Additionally, the warnings and other things that the disillusioned returning missionaries say and write about Aviabron keep coming true."

"What do they say?" asked Leyla.

"That there will be increasing outrages from Aviabron. They will be little at first and then bigger later. Those who deal with Aviabron insist there is a coming conflict," answered Sadra.

The priests and Messenger Platoon Six continued to walk slowly toward what Harold presumed was the location of New Lydia's government. Sadra continued to speak. "The Secular Authority House has a large faction, fortunately not ascendant politically as yet, that believes the Bavianer should be supported like they are in Santa Fe. The problem is that a great many of our Ancient Faith have embarked on a theological concept that it is humanity's duty on Illissos to support the Bavianer by integrating them into our culture and society."

"Yes," interrupted Harold, "I've heard all about that." He pointed to the bruises on his face.

Sadra looked at Harold curiously and then continued, "I think it is a good idea to question those using the scriptures of Ancient Faith and applying it to this new Bavianer policy. It is certainly a very bad idea to mix religious certainty with one policy or another. What appears to be noble, humane, and fair could very well be wrongheaded."

The group was walking along a large cobblestone road, and Sadra pointed to an intersecting cobblestone road, "Come this way. The Privy Council meeting will start shortly, and it isn't too much farther."

The red-robed priests surrounded the travelers, and they hurried along. The sky above them was more dazzling than in Hattusa. The area through which Harold and the others were walking was positioned on a high ridge, so much of New Lydia could be seen spreading out below. The lights from the houses created an illusion of diamonds floating around a blue sapphire lake. Above the lake was the planet Boreas. It appeared to be rising out of the lake. Harold, of course, knew that Boreas was fixed in the sky as Illissos didn't rotate itself and was tidally locked to its mother planet. Harold realized that the picturesque scene here was like this all the time; only the sky would alter from Fulldark to the twilights of Ascent and Descent to the brilliance of Fullday.

"This ridge was made sacred by the early settlers of New Lydia," said Sadra. "The view is wonderful and holy. The street we are walking on was part of the original wall of the fort the original pioneers built when humanity came to this moon. Over there"—Sadra pointed—"is the sacred stone circle and the Secular Authority House ..."

Suddenly, Greamand let out a lout cry, and then everyone heard a gurgling noise. The red-robed priest with the ice-blue eyes had sunk a knife into Greamand's back. The knife had pierced Greamand's lung, and air was rushing from the wound. The priest turned the knife, while he did so, his face was twisted in hatred and rage, and the muscles on his arms quivered.

Instantly, Harold was swept with a hateful, murderous rage that lodged midway up his throat. His muscles tightened, and his arms filled with a dark, angry energy he'd never felt before. He turned around and drove his right fist into the head of the priest. It connected with a muffled thud. The other priests, as well as Murdo, grabbed the rogue priest's arms and pulled the man away from Greamand. The man's knife was long, and it curved upward into a point. He dropped the knife on the cobblestone road. It made an evil clanging noise, and blood splattered about.

"Yetzra!" shouted Sadra. "Why?"

"This is a holy act," said Yetzra. He looked back at Sadra, Harold, and the others without flinching. His ice-blue eyes danced with frenzied certainty.

"I bring this man down to keep the peace on our moon," said Yetzra. He drew a breath and said in a loud voice, not unlike that of the high priestess of Santa Fe, "We can keep the diverse mosaic of Illissos functioning. Remember, Sadra, I am a diplomat from Santa Fe. I am immune to your city's laws." The two priests holding Yetzra's arms let go of him. Yetzra's hands were bloody, and he raised them to the sky. "A holy act," he said again.

"You rat," said Murdo. He made a fist and started for Yetzra.

Sadra and the other priests held him back.

"He has immunity," said Sadra. "We must let him go."

"Know this, Sadra," said Yetzra, "one day I will be a high priest, and I will erase your name from the Holy Annals of Priests. Peace will be maintained, and the Ancient Faith will triumph in its growth, no matter what *he* thinks and no matter what *he* tells *your* Secular Authority." Yetzra looked at Greamand lying in his own blood. He then turned and walked away with slow, calm steps. He walked as though he was in a park.

"What sort of priests are you?" asked Murdo.

"I'm sorry," replied Sadra. "Yetzra was on loan to my office from Santa Fe. I've never been comfortable with him, but I didn't expect him to do what he did. He was part of an exchange between New Lydia and Santa Fe as part of an effort to reconcile the growing schism in our Ancient Faith."

"It seems that your opposition is far more committed to their vision than you are," said Harold. "They are willing to use violence and treachery even when they are outnumbered.

Had more of your entourage been from Santa Fe, we'd all be dead now."

Greamand made a groan. It was not an ordinary groan but, instead, an eerie animal noise that a human makes when it is in extreme pain. It was a noise like no other, and Harold realized that Greamand was mortally wounded. Yetzra had done his work well. Greamand didn't have long to live.

Sadra bent down over Greamand. "My old friend," he said, "you could have just as easily been a high priest."

"Ah," said Greamand. "Would to the gods I hadn't done it."

Greamand started to sputter blood from his mouth, and his eyes looked off, far off as though he could see through the blue clouds of Boreas to the central core of the gas giant.

One of the priests was calling for an ambulance on his comms device, but everyone knew it was hopeless.

Greamand rallied and turned his eyes on Harold. "Harold," said Greamand, "you must deliver the two dispatches from Mayor Winchurst to Chairman Somerset of the Secular Authority for me."

Harold nodded.

"You need a shave too," Greamand said. He started to say more, and all leaned in to listen, but Greamand died without finishing his message.

Harold reached into Greamand's clothing and took the dispatches.

Leyla looked at Greamand with sadness. Sadra said a quiet prayer over Greamand's body. The other priests looked down, doing nothing.

Murdo, however, was quaking with rage. "You let that murderer go," said Murdo as he watched Yetzra continue to walk slowly away, as though he was a king. "You are clinging to a form of laws and morals that your opposition ignores. You are played for fools."

A priest, without a word, moved in front of Murdo to keep him from throwing a punch at Sadra or chasing after Yetzra.

"Indeed," replied Sadra. "I don't have any excuses that I can offer, but there will be no more attacks. When we get to the Secular Authority House, you will be surrounded by loyal patriots of New Lydia. There are many there and within the priesthood who bitterly regretted Greamand's exile." Sadra looked down at the dead ex-priest and said, "You were right all along, my friend."

Harold wasn't sure exactly what Greamand had been right about but figured Sadra meant Greamand's ideas on Bavianer policy.

The police and ambulance arrived, and they took Greamand's body away. The policeman could only shake his head when the group told him the situation. Yetzra was not only free to return to Santa Fe; he could remain in New Lydia until declared persona non grata by both the secular and religious authorities.

With heavy hearts, the priests and the remainder of Messenger Platoon Six continued on their way. It wasn't long before they reached the front entrance of the Secular Authority House. The house was carved from living rock. Its front entrance consisted of Corinthian columns, whose ornate tops gracefully blended into the natural stone above it. Inside, the open foyer was well lit, with marble tile for a floor. Two stairways led to a second floor. Sadra and the priests led the three to a room whose door was under the stairs.

In the room was Chairman Somerset. He was dressed in a plain, russet felt suit with a modest ruffle at the neck. He was seated at the head of a table. At the table were other men, dressed to the same level of formality.

"Welcome to the Privy Council, Sadra," said the chairman. "Who do you have with you?"

Sadra made introductions and explained what had happened. Then he nodded at Harold to formally deliver the message.

"Mr. Chairman," Harold said, "I am one of a group of messengers from Hattusa. I am tasked by the mayor to formally request military assistance due to a swarm of Bavianer who have besieged our town."

Harold looked around. Leyla and Murdo were looking at him intensely. He hadn't expected to make the formal request, and he wasn't sure exactly what to say after he explained the basics of the situation. He looked as Sadra, who nodded encouragement. Harold thought very carefully about what to say next. Greamand had wanted to personally deliver the dispatches to ensure that New Lydia committed to armed aid. Did he need to do more persuading? Did he need to make a passionate speech?

Harold decided to stick with the facts, "Mayor Winchurst has given us two dispatches. One I am to give to you. The other I am to read in the streets to plead for assistance if necessary." Harold took one of the dispatches. It had bloody fingerprints on it, prints Greamand made from his own blood.

Chairman Somerset took the dispatch with both of his hands. "Thank you," he said. The chairman opened the dispatch and read it very carefully. The chairman kept a straight face as he read, but he held his lips tight. When he finished, he put the dispatch down with shaking hands.

"Can I see it?" asked a well-dressed man in the council.

The chairman nodded.

The man picked it up, and other Privy Council members read over his shoulder. The men's eyes grew wide.

"It is just what I've been saying," said a black haired, black bearded man in a Lincoln green felt robe. "It is just what I've been saying. This situation on Illissos is unstable. The Bavianer, the settlement at Aviabron, and the political frictions in the three cities ..." Here he trailed off and a different man interrupted him.

"The conflict is set. It is now time for action," the other man said. This man was wearing a mustard brown coat. What struck Harold about him was that this man hadn't read the dispatch at all; yet he had immediately advocated action.

An argument between the men in the Privy Council erupted.

"Remember, we have many older voters who are still angry about the Mithras Heresy, which so many of those in Hattusa followed," said a man in a purple Cap of Faith.

"That was forty-five Boreas years ago," answered another man.

"I don't think the older voters will see their kith and kin butchered by a schism from that far back," answered yet another Privy Council member.

"Yes, but the water purification policy at Hattusa!" answered the man in the purple Cap of Faith. "They really burned our delegation over that. Those insults are still fresh, not five Boreas years old, and the algae blooms on the southwest side of the lake have only gotten bigger."

Chairman Somerset stood, calmed the group, and said, "We can get great leverage in our Hattusa dealings if we help them in their hour of need now." Somerset looked at Harold and said, "Thank you, young man." He then turned to the Privy Council. "The tactical situation, the combat, the war—that is what matters. In this dispatch, we haven't heard anything that we didn't already know—or at least suspect—but we have been formally charged with coming to Hattusa's aid. There are three questions here. First, should we help Hattusa? Second, can we help Hattusa? Third, how do we help Hattusa?"

The chairman turned to one man and said, "Ministry of War?"

The minister of war leaned forward. Up until now, he hadn't said anything, and Harold hadn't noticed him at all. The minister of war was not a large man; he had thin, graying hair, which appeared to have once been red, but time had taken its toll. Crow's feet lined the corners of his eyes. His face was grave. He took a breath and said in a steady voice, "To the second question, yes we can help Hattusa, and quickly. The quick way to help Hattusa is to gather the militia, put them on Zeppelins, and fly them over the mountains to directly engage the Bavianer." He then paused, looked around, and said, "*Should* we help is the wrong word. We must help Hattusa. It comes down to the fundamental eternal interests of New Lydia. First, the people of Hattusa are our own kind. We understand them. We can easily trade with them, and, in future, we can unite with them politically. Additionally, they are situated in a spot where they could control the flow of the Mighty River. If the river gets diverted there, the river here will become a dry gulley."

Harold found that the logic of the minister of war was outstanding. He felt a great relief that this was nearly over. All their sacrifice was going to be worth it. Leyla grabbed Harold's hand and squeezed it.

Chairman Somerset held up his hand. "How do you know that our militia won't get destroyed like what happened to the Hattusa militia? Remember that Aviabron—or at least the filibusters involved in this fray—have proven to have really thought this out. I've seen the report from the police interrogation on the two men who shot up the train. Those men were trained by Aviabron's allies on Earth and were mercenaries on the conflict between humans and the Krakatorians on Lugus. No doubt the fact that they were arrested by our police is known to those in Aviabron. I suspect that the filibusters surrounding Hattusa will get word from those in Aviabron who support their cause that a message has gone through."

The minister of war nodded and said, "There are always risks in these operations, but I have a hunch that the Bavianer-Aviabron alliance of the besiegers of Hattusa is already wearing thin. As far as I know, Hattusa hasn't yet fallen to its attackers. Additionally, we have one critical advantage—the Zeppelins. Right now, they are off transporting ore mined from the other moons. Under law, they can be summoned back to Illissos during an emergency. There is also one Zeppelin that we've outfitted to hold single, highly accurate cannon with ammunition. That ship can be used for fire support. I've long believed that air power will give us the edge. We can be moving by Ascent. We need to send out the call to gather the militia at the town commons. We need to broadcast on the radio that we are going to take the train to Santa Fe and then go overland to Hattusa. We need to get into a diplomatic argument with High Priestess Shazeef, who will not want us to travel through her city. Meanwhile, the Zeppelins pick up the troops, fly over, and we land on the besiegers' head. With the armed Zeppelin above and the men landing in mass on the ground, we'll take the starch right out of them."

"It's still risky," said the chairman, "but we can't lose the water."

The questions and discussion in the Privy Council became fast. How many Zeppelins could be available by

Ascent? Could they bring horses? How many shells could the armed Zeppelin fire? How would diplomatic relations with Aviabron be affected? What would the operation cost?

The chairman dismissed the travelers as the questions started to fly. A gray-robed clerk escorted the three to an outer room in the Secular Authority House, while the official, detailed plan was made by the New Lydian government.

Chapter 13

THE PREPARATIONS IN NEW LYDIA

The outer room Messenger Platoon Six occupied was well lit, white walled, and empty except for a few chairs.

"Well," said Murdo, "once I see New Lydian troops depart for Hattusa, I'm off for home."

"You mean you aren't going to join them?" asked Harold.

"No, I've done my duty," replied Murdo. "Frankly, I have a family to feed. I feel like my obligation to the mission is over. Besides, I should attend to Greamand's remains. He should be decently buried."

Harold looked at Murdo and then Leyla. "Whatever happens, I'm going with the New Lydia Militia, even if I have to stow away in a Zeppelin. However, don't think that the New Lydia militia will stop me from joining like the Hattusa Militia did."

"I wonder what Greamand would say about this situation," said Murdo.

"Whatever do you mean?" asked Leyla.

"I mean," answered Murdo, "if Harold had joined the militia when the siege first started, or if he'd left the city on his own to join them, he'd be dead now and no use to anyone. It seems the wheel of fate was on Harold's side in all this. It would be nice to know what Greamand would say. I'd have liked to hear it. He had an understanding of these matters."

Then, from the room where the Privy Council was being held, came the sounds of a song. Harold knew it well; it was a peppy hymn long sung by those of the Ancient Faith. Harold couldn't help but sing along to the catchy tune that had been taught to every schoolkid in Illissos since time immemorial.

Sadra approached the group and said, "We have the plan hammered out, the orders are cut, and the Zeppelins are recalled. We shall send forward the militia this Ascent."

"I wish to join the militia," replied Harold, "though I'll need a sword and carbine."

"Of course," answered Sadra. "You will be with our militia but will still officially be serving with Hattusa. That is," Sadra paused, "if you want to go. You have been brave enough."

"I wish to go," answered Harold.

"Young lady," Sadra said to Lydia, "you can stay as a guest of the chairman's family if you wish."

Leyla nodded yes.

"We do have some secure guest quarters for you, Harold, and Murdo in the chairman's official residence. You can rest there"—Sadra looked at Harold and continued—"as well as prepare for the attack."

Chairman Somerset joined the conversation and said, "Harold, I understand that you wish to join the attack. You'll be in Captain Benedict's company. There you'll get out outfitted with a new uniform and kit."

After this, there was a blur of activity. Because Harold was going with the militia, he was quickly whisked outside by several clerks. Outside it was still Descent, and the sky was partially bright, with the ground very dark. Normally, Descent was a time for sleeping, but once again, Harold was too excited to be tired. Adding to his wakefulness was the glow of the streetlights. Along the public walkways and streets, it seemed like Fullday.

In New Lydia, the gray-robed clerks were functionaries of the Secular Authority who managed the government's various affairs but weren't elected in their own right. The two clerks with Harold walked with an easy attitude. The men were veterans of a long ago war that New Lydia had won against the Bavianer in a suburban development around the lake. The conversation with the veteran clerks was different than any conversation Harold had ever had with an adult in Hattusa. The clerks treated Harold more like an adult. They were very impressed with Harold's retelling of the fight in the woods.

"Yeah," said one of the gray-robbed clerks, "it's strange how the Bavianer seem to be able to communicate. They can't speak with the tongue of humans, but they can manage an insult with body language."

"They're also really fast moving," added the other clerk.

"They are indeed," replied Harold. "It's important to me to get a sword. I understand they can be purchased here in New Lydia."

The clerks looked at each other. "Yes," said one, "you can get a sword. But will you really need it?"

"Yes," said Harold, "I could have used a sword several times by now. Bavianer can get awfully close. But if you have a sword, those creatures being close doesn't matter. They just get chopped with it."

The two clerks looked at each other again and shrugged.

The sword smith's shop was back toward the train station. Inside was a portly man with a leather apron. His head was shaved, but the man had on his cheeks the largest sideburns that Harold had ever seen.

"You're the young fellow from Hattusa?" asked the sword smith. "I got a call about you from the high priest."

"Yes," replied Harold. "I've come to get a cavalry saber—a shashka-style saber."

"Like the ones that the Hattusa militia buys?" asked the sword smith.

"Yes, sir, I'm from Hattusa," answered Harold.

"Plenty of goings-on there. It has been announced that our troops are going to attack the Bavianer. They are going to take the train to Santa Fe and then go overland."

Harold knew that to be incorrect, but he kept his mouth shut. He didn't want to give away the secret that they would attack using Zeppelins. The secret, however, really wanted to break out. The sword smith must have seen some pained expression on Harold's face.

"Something troubling you?" asked the sword smith.

Harold thought about what to say, and then said, "My family is in Hattusa. I fear for them. I really need a sword."

"You know," replied the sword smith, "most of the New Lydia militia gets a short stabbing sword. They put it on the side of their backpack and use it for more than just stabbing. They can cut brush and dig a bit with it. It's more of a tool. You folks in Hattusa are the only ones who really use a sword for just warfare.

"I really want the saber," answered Harold. "We're always mounted on the frontier, and the Bavianer fights won't end for a while." In his mind, Harold looked ahead toward the future with a fearful certainty. Conflict between the civilized and the uncivilized would be a constant. In this condition, peace is either a farce carried out by people like High Priestess Shazeef or a temporary aberration. If one fed the Bavianer, they multiplied; if you didn't feed them, they only became more dangerous. If one declared equality with them as sentient beings, the equality itself would be a transparent lie. The Bavianer would just be able to dance in time to music while restrained. There was no way to equally yoke the civilizationally competent with such wild beasts. The humans on Illissos, those of the Ancient Faith who had started their journey on the hills of northwestern England, were now locked in a never-ending battle. There was nothing more to do but fight to win.

"Might as well face up to it," said Harold while thinking of the fight out loud.

"What was that?" asked the sword smith.

"Nothing," said Harold.

One of the gray-robed clerks spoke up. "Put the cost of the sword on the Secular Authority tab."

"I can have you a saber in several hours," said the smith. "I can have it delivered."

Harold was also given a New Lydia Militia uniform. The uniform was heavy-duty woven cloth, and the two stripes indicating his rank were made of felt. The pants and tunic were Illissos beige, and the tunic bore a flash on the shoulder that said Hattusa. Also with the uniform was a pistol belt with two suspenders, as well as a steel helmet. At the guest quarters, Harold took a long shower and changed into his uniform. The boots were stiff and new. Feeling clean and wearing clean clothes were wonderful. Until this journey, Harold never really appreciated a hot shower and laundered clothes. When he looked at himself in the mirror, he was quite pleased. But the scruffy whiskers on his cheeks were out of place. Militiamen were always shaved.

A knock at the door interrupted his thoughts. It was Sadra, Leyla, and Murdo. "You need a shave," said Sadra. In the high priest's hand was a straight razor. Harold sat down.

"Normally," said Sadra, "a boy's mother, aunt, or sister applies the shaving cream to the face of a boy who has come to manhood. In this case, Leyla will be a substitute."

Leyla took a shaving soap brush from Sadra and applied the shaving cream to Harold's face. Leyla didn't look directly into Harold's eyes as she applied the shaving cream. Instead she focused on applying the cream with the greatest of concentration. Her eyes were radiant, blue like the planet Boreas on a clear Fulldark.

When she finished, Sadra spoke, "Do you, Harold, join the Ancient Faith as a man?"

"Yes," replied Harold.

"Then, I shave your beard, which has just grown in." Sadra took the straight razor and plied it across Harold's face.

Harold was glad that he was getting shaved when the whiskers on his face were really just a bit more than heavy fuzz. Others he'd known had had quite thick beards by the time they'd received their first shave, and the process had taken much longer, with some wincing on the part of the man getting shaved.

When Sadra finished, he said, "Rise, new man. Walk and grow in the Ancient Faith."

Everyone in the room clapped and shook Harold's hand. Leyla gave Harold a hug.

Then there was a knock at the door. The two clerks had come, along with a man carrying the sword Harold had ordered.

"Harold, sir," the deliveryman said, "my name is Graham Underhill. Here is your sword."

"Thank you, sir," replied Harold. He took the sword and held it in the same way that Sergeant Burbeen had done on Hattusa. The sword was perfectly balanced. He drew the

174

sword from the scabbard, and it gleamed in the artificial light coming from the guest quarters ceiling lights.

"Looks great," said Murdo. "You'll do very well rescuing poor Hattusa with the New Lydia Militia." He then added, "That sword can last you a long time. You'll likely need it for a long time too."

Leyla looked at Harold but didn't say anything. When the Bavianer siege had started, Harold had wanted to go fight them mounted up on his camel Clem and return a hero. When that proved impossible, he'd gone on a mission that had turned out to be far more difficult and challenging than a normal Bavianer hunt. Now, he was going to return by Zeppelin to do battle with the Bavianer. He was already a hero for delivering the message, but was he headed to being a dead hero?

"It is time," said one of the gray-robed clerks. "The militia will be gathering at the Zeppelin field."

Harold said his good-bye to Leyla. He didn't quite know what to say to the beautiful girl who stood before him. She whispered to him, "I hope to see you again in Hattusa." When he hugged Leyla good-bye, a toxic mix of emotions welled up in his breast. They were a mix of longing, sadness, desire, and fear.

He went to shake Murdo's hand, but the shepherd gave him a hug instead. "I'll bring your camels back to Hattusa when the siege is lifted."

"Do you think you'll be arrested in Santa Fe?" asked Harold.

"I could be," answered Murdo, "but the Santa Fe District is my home. If I go through the North Gate, I won't run into the Bavianer forest and the security cameras. Also, nobody was really looking for me in particular in Santa Fe; the focus was on Greamand. Also, now that New Lydia is in the war and the train got shot up, the Santa Fe Seminary will have trouble getting students and aid. Nobody wants to send their kid to a place where there are shoot-ups on the train. We, the shepherds and farmers and workers of Santa Fe, will become much more valuable than the high priestess and her followers. Nobody will come after me."

Harold, led by the two gray-robed clerks, walked to the Zeppelin field. It was Ascent now; the sun was just starting to rise in the east, and the gloom of Fulldark was ending. Harold carried his new sword in the same way that Sergeant Burbeen had. He tried to be relaxed, but he was filled with an electric anticipation. The quest was nearly done—his quest. He just had to return to show everyone what he'd done. He'd be a hero. He was also a grown man. Still, this next push could end it all. The near misses that Harold had experienced while getting to New Lydia gave him chills. The next encounter might not be a miss.

Harold and the clerks passed several protestors. They were wearing the Caps of Faith and had signs that said, "Santa Fe is *not* just a throughway to violence," and, "Ban Hate, Not Bavianer!" But these protestors were few. On the whole, the streets were empty.

At the Zeppelin field, the militia was assembling. Troops were forming up into little groups, and the families gathered around the edges of the formations. One of the clerks stopped Harold and said, "It's time to join your company. Remember that you are more experienced than most of the men in the militia in Bavianer fighting, but it is best to be humble. You're pretty young. Don't brag about your rank. There are older men than you with lower rank. They'll resent your two stripes. Also, the Secular Authority put out a story that the militia was assembling at the Zeppelin field and would march to the train station. What will really happen is that three Zeppelins, one armed with cannon, will land, and the militia will fly to Hattusa. It will be a surprise attack from the air."

Of course, Harold already knew this, but in the spirit of being humble, he didn't say anything. Harold thought back to his last argument with his mother; he'd have argued with her if she'd said something like what the wise veteran had just told him, but now Harold knew, or had the maturity to recognize, that the veteran was saying something important, something with a ring of mature, hard-won truth.

As Harold approached the militiamen, red-robed priests and gray-robed clerks began to shoo the families away from the gathering soldiers. The officers and sergeants shouted orders. One of the clerks directed Harold to a tall officer. "This is Captain Benedict. You will be in his company."

Captain Benedict showed him to a machine gun crew. His job would be to help carry the ammunition and provide security with his rifle and sword for the crew. The rest of the men had all sorts of equipment—there were radios; backpacks; and short, stabbing swords attached to backpacks. Some of the men had special optics attached to their helmets to better see in the twilight conditions. Harold's rifle had the same optics as part of the sight.

Then suddenly, three Zeppelins appeared above them. They made no noise at all. Harold would find out later that the miners who'd been using the Zeppelins had had to hastily dump the ore they'd collected from the outer moons and were none too happy. They were covered in the dust of those moons, and the shine from the aluminum skin peeked out from behind a thin, beige gauzelike layer of dirt.

The Zeppelins were called such because they looked much like the early heavier-than-air vehicles used in the early twentieth century. The look, however, was not based on nostalgia. Instead, the large bulge above the passenger and crew was where the antigravity engines were housed. The larger the antigravity engine, the quicker and lighter the Zeppelin could be. A Zeppelin could roar off the surface of Illissos, go to the various moons of Boreas, and land as gently as a feather, fully loaded with ore.

Harold was introduced to the machine gun team and given a rough outline of the plan of attack; his company was to land on a hill and clear the area to the city wall of any and all Bavianer and Aviabron humans. Harold knew the area they would attack. It was the same patch of ground over which Messenger Platoon Six made their escape out of the city. (Harold felt his eyes sting as he thought of his late wise friend and hoped Greamand would be happy the message had worked.) The other side of the city was to be captured by a different company landing closer to the river.

In addition to his sword, kit, and rifle, Harold was given two boxes of machine gun ammunition to carry. After the plan was fully explained and the men had conducted their rehearsals, Harold and his company went to board the closest Zeppelin.

Chapter 14

THE ASSAULT BY ZEPPELIN

Harold entered the Zeppelin. The interior cabin of the troop compartment was spacious and well lit. The benches consisted of a steel frame with red nylon canvas stretched across the frame. The men sat down on the benches and put their gear in various places, like under the bench or underfoot, like footrests. Harold was positioned next to a window, and so he was able to watch the liftoff. The Zeppelin took off from the field and began to move away from the city.

To Harold, it didn't feel like he was flying. Instead, the ground seemed to fall away, and the buildings that made up the city of New Lydia passed below in a blur. Soon the Zeppelin was very high, in the darkness of space.

Captain Benedict stood and announced, "The Zeppelins are going to fly very high, above the atmosphere. When we are over our landing zone at Hattusa, we will reenter the atmosphere from above. The Zeppelin is going to a high orbit around the moon to kill time. We are killing time to allow the sun to be positioned in such a way that we will be descending out of it. That way, we'll land right on top of the Bavianer, and they won't see us coming at all. It will be Fullday when we arrive. We'll be able to see them clearly.

Harold calculated that the landing was, thus, several hours away. He looked over at the other men around him. They were all young men but older than Harold—mostly in their twenties.

"You're pretty young to be a corporal," said the squad leader, who looked to be about twenty-five years old, looking at Harold's stripes.

"I'm from Hattusa. I was made a corporal when I got here because I am a messenger from that city to New Lydia," answered Harold.

"Well aren't you something," the squad leader said cruelly.

Harold didn't know what to say and was cut by the curt answer. Apparently, he wasn't a hero in the New Lydia militia.

"Say, have you been to the area we are expected to land?" asked another man.

"Yes," answered Harold.

A couple of soldiers pulled out a map, and Harold pointed to it and told them the story of the pack mule and the layout of the enemy forces as he understood it. By now, of course, his information was somewhat out of date, but most of the company gathered around to listen anyway. Harold's big concern was the grove of trees from where the fire that killed the mule had originated. The area could have been reinforced. The company was planning to land at the edge of the enemy force's positions and then move toward the city, killing or capturing everything in the way. There was some concern that they might land in the center of the enemy position and thus be surrounded.

Soldiers headed for combat, no matter how well trained, are saddled with a very intense fear, which can take hold of one man and spread very quickly. The very idea of landing in the middle of armed humans and howling Bavianer hit upon those fears, and pretty soon several men expressed concerns in a loud way that they were "headed for a trap."

To head off the fear, Captain Benedict came by and said, "Relax; we won't be surrounded. We've thought through where the besiegers will be positioned."

The discussion went on for a while, though with less fear and more focus on the job and then tapered off after the first sergeant, a gray-haired somewhat heavy man, ordered the men tried to get some shut-eye before the fight.

With nothing to do, Harold drifted off to an uneasy sleep. The Zeppelin crew had dimmed the cabin lights, and the men became silent. Harold dreamed his feet were sticking out of the bottom of the Zeppelin, and Bavianer below were trying to grab them.

Suddenly, the lights went on and Harold was jolted awake.

Captain Benedict shouted, "Get ready. We will be landing in thirty minutes."

There was a scrambling as men stretched, got on their kits, checked their rifles, and arranged themselves for battle. Harold found that the sword was in his way, even when attached to his backpack. He also had to hold the rifle and carry two heavy boxes of ammunition. He put the rifle's strap around his neck so the rifle would be resting in his front, ready to fire, but his hands were still free to hold ammunition boxes. Then the Zeppelin started its rapid descent from space.

For Harold, there was no sense of falling, as the antigravity was working in the troop compartment, and the men were able to stand as though they were on solid ground. Instead, there was a terrible pain in the inner part of his ears—the cabin's pressurization apparently not sufficient to keep Harold's ears from throbbing. Other men were also pulling on their ears and wincing with discomfort.

After what seemed a very long time, the pain subsided. The Zeppelin made several unexplainable jerky motions and then the back door ramp opened, revealing they were on the ground. The men piled out. Outside, there was a thick haze of smoke everywhere. It stung Harold's eyes.

Harold couldn't see anything through the haze, and matters were made worse when the Zeppelin lifted off. The soldiers on the ground were hit by a flow of air from the Zeppelin's direction—its engines created a miniature dust storm on the landing zone. A blast of what seemed like solid Earth struck Harold's eyes, blinding him temporarily. When he blinked out the dust and his sight returned, he found himself next to the machine gun crew. They had set up the gun and were firing away.

Before the first burst was finished, a platoon leader ran to them and commanded they cease fire. In the smoke and confusion of the landing, Harold's squad had started to attack in the wrong direction.

As the smoke and dust cleared, the situation did likewise. Harold helped reposition the gun. The platoon leader—Harold didn't know his name—pointed to where the machine gun should aim, but he was only just in time. Whatever surprise the company had from the Zeppelin flying in, shielded by the sun's glare, was gone. The Bavianer were rallying, and several human soldiers with rifles and radios were directing the action. The humans were wearing the same sort of uniforms that the men who'd shot up Messenger Platoon Six's cabin on the train had worn. The Aviabron humans pointed and shouted orders and then took cover, vanishing behind the scrub brush and other folds in the terrain. The Bavianer did likewise, only in larger numbers. Harold knew immediately that the creatures were advancing to his position while under cover.

Then there was a crackling flurry of bullets zipping by Harold and his machine gun crew. Harold ducked and discovered that the fire was coming from a grove of trees, the same grove of trees from which the missile or explosive charge that blew up the pack mule had originated. Now it seemed like an enemy machine gun crew had taken position there. Another burst—the bullets were closer now. The two machine gunners ducked rather than firing back. Harold ducked too.

Harold looked at the machine gun and the ducking crew. The machine gun was unmanned, sitting there, doing nothing. He thought about running to the gun and shooting back; he calculated the angle in which he'd point the gun to return fire and thought about the timing. He could shoot them, but they, obviously, could also shoot him, and they'd have the advantage of cover. It could very well be a suicide mission.

All the sounds of the battle were silenced out by the intensity of Harold's thinking. The unmanned machine gun stood in the center of Harold's vision. He could see the dust from the bullets kick up around it. Harold could look at the gun, but his mind seemed to be stuck, unable to send a message to his body to move.

One of the men in his machine gun crew was hit. It was the sergeant who had been so sharp with Harold on the Zeppelin. Then suddenly, several explosions cut through Harold's concentration, and the incoming bullets stopped hitting the dirt around Harold and the others. The Zeppelin with the cannon had fired on the enemy machine gun crew from the air and destroyed it.

The sounds of battle resumed, and Harold's mind became unfrozen. The wounded man made a horrible cry. His leg was shattered. There was blood everywhere. Harold cried for a medic.

And then the Bavianer were on them. Another man took the machine gun and started to fire. Harold also pointed his rifle and fired, but the few shots he managed to get out were scattered. He didn't hit any Bavianer, and they continued to advance. The machine gun stopped firing.

"More ammo!" shouted a gunner.

Harold looked down at his ammo cans and brought them to the gun. After a quick reload, the gun was back in action. The Zeppelin in the air fired down on the pack of Bavianer attacking Harold's company. The rest of the company had organized and fired away at the Aviabron humans and the Bavianer.

The company formed a line as rehearsed and began to move forward toward Hattusa's walls. The machine gunners moved to supporting positions and fired away.

Captain Benedict shouted, "The Zeppelin will soften up the enemy in front of us as we advance. Shoot the Bavianer, but try and take the humans prisoner. We need them for intelligence."

Ahead of the forward-moving company, came sharp, dusty explosions from the cannon of the Zeppelin above. After each explosion, the air, just for a whisper of a second, became like steel as the shockwave passed by him. One close blast caused Harold tremendous pain in his eardrums.

"Keep moving, men," shouted the captain. "Keep as close to the supporting fire as possible."

Harold knew that the purpose of keeping close to the artillery fire was to get in close to the enemy while the enemy was ducking the cannon fire and unable to mount an effective resistance, but the company was awfully close to the explosions ...

And then a roaring sound and a fierce, close blast, which drowned out everything else. Harold let out an involuntary cry, and his uniform felt like thousands of hooks were grasping at it as the shock wave passed. It was an explosion from the supporting shell, too close this time. To his left there were shouts and firing. A Bavianer—hidden from above—had been gunned down by the infantry on the ground; apparently the creature had been flushed out of hiding by the last close blast.

The company was making good progress. The Zeppelin had landed in the right spot—just on the edge of where the Aviabron humans and their Bavianer allies had taken positions. Therefore, the company wasn't surrounded, and every step forward toward Hattusa was one step closer to victory.

On Harold's left was a line of trees. He kept looking toward it and then back to the area forward of the company. As they advanced, they came upon the corpses of the Bavianer. Some were in pieces—they'd been shattered by cannon fire. Some had died in agony from the injuries caused by bullet wounds. All the dead were covered in a thin layer of dust. It seemed that once life left a body in the dry dust of Illissos, the desert moved to reclaim the dead.

A passage from the Scriptures of the Ancient Faith played in Harold's mind, unbidden: *Man came from dust and will return to dust.*

Harold continued to advance. He passed a scrub bush, and there was an Aviabron human. The man on the ground was barely alive. A female Bavianer was above him, and the doe Bavianer was holding a nursing cub. Harold expected her to lunge at Harold, but incredibly, she bent down and began to eat the face from the living Aviabroner. There was a sort of muffled cry from the unfortunate soldier and then a crunch as the Bavianer crushed the man's skull with her powerful jaws.

It was sickening. Harold dropped his ammunition can and pointed his rifle to fire, but then to his horror, he realized the rifle was out of bullets. He reached toward his backpack and drew the sword. It was a slow, fumbling draw. Harold had strapped the sword to his backpack but not in such a way that it could easily be drawn. The Bavianer finished off the head of the Aviabroner in several bites. The dead, headless soldier twitched for a bit and then lay still. The doe Bavianer's eyes drifted over to Harold, and they held an almost human reflection in them, but they were human only in the sense of a dull, half-understanding. The half-understanding was mixed with a look in her eyes that was also cruel and empty.

The sword was out. The Bavianer had, amazingly, not pounced and was still dull and listless. Harold wondered if the Aviabron humans were giving the Bavianer drugs to make them controllable in some way but unpredictable and listless in another. The fur on the Bavianer's black face was stained with the human's blood. The creature's lips were red, and her teeth were sharp and long. Harold raised the sword and brought it down.

The sword slashed off the arm of the female and killed the nursing baby. The Bavianer looked at the dead cub and looked at Harold. She made an expression of clear sorrow. Immediately, Harold felt a strong sympathy for the creature. She didn't really seem to care about her missing arm. Instead, to Harold, it seemed that she only felt a wild mother's longing for the dead baby. *It must be those expressions*, thought Harold, *which helped prompt Shazeef on her Bavianer policies.* In that moment, Harold also realized one thing about the Bavianer. The empty and cruel look, followed by the look that expressed a childish sorrow meant the Bavianer could only be at your throat or at your feet. Managing Bavianer meant managing the misguided desire for mercy to them as much as it meant developing weapons and combat strategy.

Harold drew in a great breath and swung again. The Bavianer's head neatly separated from the rest of its body. Harold had no idea of his own strength—the sword worked wonderfully.

"Good job, man," said Captain Benedict.

The radio operator behind him was beaming a smile. Then, an explosion came—it was the same sort of explosion that had taken out the mule. Only this time, it killed the radio operator. Harold's machine gun crew, just to his right, returned fire—though at what Harold couldn't see.

Harold looked down at the dead radio operator. An instant before, he had been alive and standing; now his body was covered with a thin layer of dust, and two small trickles of blood emerged, one from each of the dead man's ears.

"Take over as radio operator," said the captain dryly.

There was a flurry of pushing and heaving from the other men to get the radio off the deceased soldier. Harold gave the other machine gun ammunition can to the crew, dropped his pack, and saddled the radio on his back.

"On the radio," said Captain Benedict, "I'm Echo Six. You listen to the radio, and when I reach out my hand, you press the hand mic into my hand. Understand?"

"Yes, sir," said Harold.

The roar of battle continued. Captain Benedict held out his hand. Harold pressed the radio into his hands. The radio itself was pretty heavy. In the transfer of pack and ammo, Harold had wedged his sword and scabbard into part of the radio so he could continue to carry the weapon, but now he couldn't draw it without taking the radio pack off. Harold realized that, in these circumstances, a sword was less than ideal.

He put another magazine into his rifle and looked around. Captain Benedict was ordering the platoon on the far left to enter the grove of cottonwood trees and clear out what was there. The rest of the company was to provide a cross fire and lift and shift as ordered. Initially, Harold didn't understand what that meant, but the men in the company had done the drill before. The machine gun crew blasted away at the forest just in front of the advancing platoon on the left. Eventually there was a call on the radio. An Aviabron human had been captured.

Captain Benedict directed Harold to inform the New Lydians on the other side of Hattusa that he was going to close in toward "Objective Echo." That was the gate through which Harold, Greamand, and Murdo had escaped from Hattusa. Captain Benedict wanted the armed Zeppelin to return and look over the area to his immediate front in case more hidden Bavianer could be shot from the air.

Immediately, however, the higher-ranking officer from the New Lydia Militia attacking "Objective Able" on the front gate jumped in the conversation and insisted that he needed the armed support. The argument between the two officers raged until the pilot on the Zeppelin said he could see both sides of Hattusa. No Bavianer were hiding immediately in front of Captain Benedict's company, and the company could "proceed to Objective Echo."

With some cursing, the men were back on their feet and moving forward. The Zeppelin above made several shots from its cannon, but the cannon gunners were firing in support of the New Lydians on the other side of town. Harold looked at the big iron craft so far away and high and wondered exactly how the pilot could truly see both sides of the city.

The telltale Bavianer snarl came from the right. Harold looked that direction, and a Bavianer pounced on a man. But in a second, some other New Lydian had killed the Bavianer. Naturally, a cry for the medic ensued. Every clash he'd seen so far had been like this—not one had come to a clean, heroic end, with a dead Bavianer and a human warrior of the Ancient Faith glowing with victory. Instead, every fight had ended with blood and injury on both sides.

The company continued to advance. When the company reached the walls, Captain Benedict called on the radio. "We've cleared our area and have reached the gate at Objective Echo." He then added, "After having one more man wounded by Bavianer."

There was a response, but Harold was unable to hear anything other than a muffled, static-filled reply as the captain was holding the hand mic to his ear.

Chapter 15

Entering the Gates of Hattusa

Once Harold's company had reached the walls of Hattusa, the soldiers took up defensive positions outside the city. They were met by cheers from the older militiamen who had spent the siege guarding the walls and gates. Harold looked at them carefully. The Hattusa militiamen looked exhausted and gray. Their eyes were seemingly in a permanent squint from looking into the constant twilight. Though the men were smiling on the surface, their eyes expressed despair.

Orders came down on the radio. Harold passed the message to Captain Benedict, who acknowledged it and then gave orders to "consolidate and set up a defensive perimeter."

This order turned out to have all sorts of implications. The machine guns had to be sighted in, and some of the older men, sergeants, arranged interlocking fields of fire. The wounded were collected in one place for evacuation by Zeppelin. Harold had to turn over his radio duties to another and go back to the battlefield to find the backpack he had dropped. It was more difficult to find than he'd expected, since he'd dropped it after killing the Bavianer mother and her cub, right next to a scrub bush that turned out to look like all the other Illissos scrub bushes.

When he finally located the spot, he looked upon the remains of the scene of horror. The blood from the decapitated human had pooled above the ragged neck stump sticking above the shoulders, and the pool was starting to draw flies. The dead Bavianer mother was still situated over the Aviabron soldier, and her dead cub looked lifelessly up at Boreas.

Harold thought about pulling the dead Bavianer off the human but then decided to just leave the bodies as they were. The human had thrown his lot in with beasts; his mortal remains might as well be under them. Eventually, the scavengers and carrion hover-birds would turn the dead to bones—that is, unless there was a burial party.

And Harold decided to not bury the man himself or volunteer for a burial detail.

When Harold returned, there was little to do but return to his radio-telephone operator duty and listen on the radio to the New Lydia Militia's mopping-up efforts. Either more Bavianer had been on the other side of the city or those there had been better hidden. The men on the ground would hiss out the location of a group of Bavianer, and with clinical detachment, the targeting team on an armed Zeppelin would relay back the method of firing. The sound of the explosions reached the ears of Harold and the other men with a little delay after the announcement on the radio indicated rounds had been fired. Eventually the battle turned into a three-hour hunt for a pack of Bavianer that dodged and hid from the New Lydians in the underbrush near the river.

Finally, Captain Benedict became impatient with sitting around holding a defensive position. He ordered a platoon to move to the area near the river to help out. Harold volunteered for this duty. He again passed the radio off to another man and joined the attackers.

After a quick consulting of a map, the men moved off toward the sound of the guns. When they got to the spot across the river from where they supposed the Bavianer would be, they saw nothing except craters where the Zeppelin had fired. The lack of body parts indicated the Zeppelin had fired in vain.

Over the last two Orbweeks, Harold's instincts as to where the Bavianer would be had been honed well. He figured that the Bavianer were moving downstream just along the riverbank in the high reeds. He sniffed the air for the oil refinery smell of the beasts—nothing. Then, he saw one, in the reeds.

"There," shouted Harold. He fired.

A horrid screech of anger rang out. Harold wasn't sure if he'd hit the creature or merely enraged it.

The rest of the men began to fire at the Bavianer. The tracers made a reflection as they passed over the water of the Mighty River. Every now and then a tracer bullet would strike the river and skip like a stone. Above, the Zeppelin gunners saw the firing, and fired themselves. The blast from three explosive shells stabbed at Harold's ears. The New Lydians across the river closed in on the area and finished off the pack, and the battle was declared won. And they had finished just as Fullday was ending. The shadows were long, the sun low.

With the conclusion of the fighting, the men marched into Hattusa in victory.

The city itself was eerie and smaller than Harold had remembered it before. It was eerie in that the city was quite dark. He would later learn that the Aviabroners had fired precision-guided rockets to destroy the electrical grid as the siege went on. The faces of the Hattusa citizens looked tiredly at the marching relief force. A smattering of clapping and cheering greeted the forces, but on the whole, the celebrations were subdued. Harold noticed the young women were not out on the streets. He would later learn that rumors in the city had in that the New Lydians might be as bad for Hattusa as Aviabron, so many of the girls were hidden in lofts and attics and other secret places. The mistrust within the three city-states was still in effect, even though New Lydia's leaders had rushed to help the moment they understood the situation.

When the New Lydia Militia got to the Hattusa commons, Harold saw that the sacred fire continued to burn. Its glow cut into the gathering gloom of Descent. The sacred stone circle was decorated in yellow ribbons and flowers. Harold would later discover that, throughout the siege, the women of the town had decorated the gray stones to honor their dead brothers, sons, and fathers—the militiamen who had been killed.

The New Lydians assembled at the commons. After a while, the officers met with Mayor Winchurst and High Priestess Bogedet. Harold looked at the heavyset priestess with a shudder. He knew that he'd never be able to look at one of those red-robed women the same after his time in the Santa Fe prison. The high priestess staggered and swayed a bit. She looked a bit drunk.

The mayor went to the portico. He said some words of thanks, but most of the words didn't reach Harold's ears. The words of the mayor's speech vanished in the twilight as though the gloomy darkness could swallow sound as easily as light.

Captain Benedict told the men to "fall out" and the men milled about. By now many of the citizens of Hattusa had gathered on the commons and were starting to show some warmth to the New Lydian men. There were handshakes and hugs.

Captain Benedict called Harold over. "Young man," the captain said, "you've done a hell of a fine job. Mayor Winchurst says he sent out several groups of messengers. You seem to be the only one who made it. As of now, you're free to go back home. You've done your duty. Most of the men are going to go back to New Lydia by Zeppelin this very Descent, but we are leaving a platoon to help bury the Hattusa Militia next Fullday. As of now, the gates to the city are open, and people are free to return to their farms and homes."

Harold liked the sound of that. Then, Harold's mother, Gladys, and his two sisters rushed to him.

"You've shaved," said Gladys. She was wearing a different dress than the one she'd had on when he left. It was blue and white—not felt, just the twill weave of the working people. Harold noticed that his mother seemed smaller than before and considerably older. It was as though the strain of worry under which she'd spent the siege had been so heavy it had physically pushed her toward the ground.

Harold expected Mayor Winchurst to personally thank him for his efforts, but the mayor never so much as came onto the field to shake his hand. Instead, he disappeared off the portico. Many weeks later, Harold would discover that the mayor had been busy ensuring that electronic communications between Hattusa and the rest of Illissos was restored with some of the equipment the New Lydians had brought.

Additionally, the mayor personally met with the captured Aviabron human. The captured prisoner had confirmed what Greamand had said all along. He was a filibuster, who had joined up with the besiegers on a lark of sorts. Although Aviabron had enough water, there was a small but powerful faction of Aviabroners who saw the diverting of the Mighty as a fulfillment of, if not religious prophecy, their immediate hopes and dreams for financial gain. The large, dry expanse to the west of Aviabron would be turned into an irrigation canal-watered garden. They were going to take the desert and call it Babylon; it was to blossom as the rose.

Epilogue

It was later agreed to put the captured Aviabroner on trial, but showing exactly what crime the man had been involved in proved quite difficult. The city of Hattusa had no law against supporting a Bavianer siege. Moreover, the only evidence against the filibuster was that he'd been captured by the New Lydians when they'd broken the siege. Hattusa's prosecutors could present no proof he'd committed murder, and technically, the Santa Fe–based defense lawyers argued, he was a uniformed prisoner of war. The Aviabron human himself insisted that he hadn't been part of the group that had ambushed the Hattusa cavalry; he'd only arrived at the siege on the last day and then only carried messages. It seemed he was going to get off.

Other Aviabron humans had been killed, either by the militia or by the Bavianer, who'd turned on their human partners when the New Lydians had shown up. A good portion of the other Aviabron filibusters, perhaps most, had escaped when they'd seen that the tide of battle had decisively turned. Harold figured that the men who had occupied his farmhouse had seen the Zeppelins and done exactly that.

During the prime viewing hours at Ascent and Descent, the TV news shows followed the ins and outs of the legal issues involving the captured man. The show *Grace & Justice* was by far the most concerned over the trial. The show itself became, as they say on Illissos, an "overgloom hit" on the news channel. The show's hostess, Miss Grace Morgan, had previously held a small role on a game show. On that show, she had just smiled and spun a roulette wheel. As a hostess on her own show, Miss Grace was always addressed as *Miss*, for she had lost her fiancé in the siege and vowed revenge. Her singleness was part of her martyrdom act. Miss Grace was quite witty, and her monologues were followed by most of the city.

Harold viewed the controversy with little passion. Try as he might, he didn't feel any intense feelings one way or the other. Much of the hatred he'd felt toward the Aviabron humans had been expunged when he'd killed the doe Bavianer and her cub after the female had killed the injured Aviabroner. The horror of the entangled mess of death still lingered in his mind. Even with his ambivalence, Harold knew he wouldn't object to the prisoner being hanged.

In the end, it didn't matter at all what Harold thought. The captured Aviabron human met his fate when group of Hattusan women stormed the prison, grabbed the captive, and hacked him to death with swords. The women were widows from the siege, and they'd taken the swords from the bodies of the slain when the people of Hattusa had gone to bury and collect their dead men. After the hacking incident, *Grace & Justice* shifted focus to the menace of alcohol at support-group meetings.

After ... it seemed to Harold that things were divided into before and after the siege. Before the siege—and to be truthful, even as Harold had boarded the Zeppelin and marched with the New Lydians —Harold had imagined that he would return and be proclaimed a hero. This hadn't really occurred, although some people, his mother and sisters, had said they were proud of him. Francis got some acclaim in that he'd helped beat back an attempt by several Aviabron humans to put a ladder against the wall for the Bavianer to scale to the top and get in one Descent. The militiamen who'd held the city were often called the "heroes on the wall." On the whole, though, the people involved in the siege who were still living were ignored. Instead, the public focused on the dead militiamen. The grief, the loss, the memory of the fathers, brothers, and sons swept to the forefront of all social considerations.

Harold was now just a man and a corporal in the militia. He worked hard on his farm, though now he saw the place as a business with its risks and rewards, rather than a place where he did chores for his mother. The big question was how to get more money out of the farm and pay all the bills. After looking over all the issues regarding borrowing money, Harold didn't feel comfortable yet doing so. His mother agreed with him, and so they stayed away from credit.

One day, four Orbweeks after the siege, Murdo came to the farm on his camels. It was Fullday, and the sun shown gloriously down on Harold's farm; Boreas was but a blue highlight on the glorious blue sky. Murdo wanted to get his dogs back, get paid for his messenger work, and buy some sheep breeding stock from the survivors of the hearty sheep that had survived outside the walls during the siege. Murdo figured that the survivors, having survived such a vicious siege, would automatically be tough and, thus, better adapted to Illissos condition. After dropping off Clem, King Faisal, and Bedouin Bit, Murdo said, "Why don't we go into town. I'll buy you a drink. You're old enough now to try some of Hattusa's finest ale."

Since the siege, Hattusa had become far more interested in public works of a defensive nature. The city government had agreed to a major project to expand the walled portion of the city to include a Zeppelin landing field with a terminal and a landing pad. This way, Zeppelin flights from New Lydia would be secure under all conditions—Zeppelin flights from New Lydia were now once an Orbweek. The New Lydians decided that they needed to protect Hattusa so that they could protect their waterway, so the weekly Zeppelin flight became a priority. Additionally, there were plans drawn up for settlements farther up the Mighty River.

As Harold passed the Zeppelin field, he gave a long look at the construction site. Survey flags mapped out the landing field and the spot where walls lined with orange flags, blinking orange lights, and large light generators would ease visibility during Fulldark and the twilight times.

The hard lessons had been learned from the siege. The comms center would be relocated to the inside of a prominent rocky area within the city. A robotic drill-and-mining kit was imported to help with the work. The project was expected to take ten Orbweeks, unless the robotic drill broke down. To pay for this, new taxes were created. Additionally, stocks were issued to expedite the building of the railroad from Santa Fe to Hattusa, although the track had yet to be laid. Harold had sold a calf to help with this and donated part of his militia wages. Selling a calf for a secure communications network and an easy train ride was considerably nicer than going on a hazardous overland quest to get help.

"I hope to make some extra money by working on the railway project," Harold said to Murdo as the subject came up in their traveling conversation.

"I'll wager you that there will be a financial scandal involving the railroad before long," replied Murdo. "That money is now in a big, easy-to-grab pot. It's only a matter of time before some crook gets ahold of it. Mark my words— one of the widows of the heroic fallen is teaming up with one of the 'heroes on the wall' to do this, and they'll get away with it." He then added, "I'd bet they'll only take some of the money, not all; they'll be clever."

At this, Harold could only laugh. As soon as the network had been fixed following the arrival of the New Lydians, a series of documentaries discussing the fallen heroes had come out. There were interviews with the various widows and profiles of the life of Colonel Caleb Shreve. Harold found the constant grief shown on TV oppressive.

The pair entered the open gate of Hattusa, dropped their camels off at the livery stable, and then proceeded to the bar and restaurant downtown.

Once they were at their table, the pitcher of ale arrived. "Murdo," said Harold, "it isn't the same these last two Orbweeks, and I think the change will be permanent."

"What do you mean?" asked Murdo.

"I think about our trip, our mission all the time now," answered Harold. "It seems that no matter what I do, I can zip right back there in my mind to those events quite suddenly. I can still see the Bavianer attacking us, chasing me on Clem. I can see the fight at the train station. Most especially, I think about the two men coming to get us on the train. I dream about them."

"Yes, I understand," answered Murdo. "We've been through an experience that nobody else has, and we are marked from it. I think I understand the Scriptures of the Ancient Faith when they said the Great Dissenter was marked after his experience on Pendle Hill."

"You're not getting religious on me now, are you?" asked Harold. "Greamand went through all that study and was an up-and-coming priest. Still, he lost his faith. Our Ancient Faith might just as well be nonsense."

"It could be," answered Murdo, "but I find it a comfort regardless. I feel now that all of this—all of this religion, politics, war, and what to do or not do—takes place in semidarkness. In that darkness, we are inconsistent and uncertain." Murdo paused. "Greamand would say this so much better than me of course. I'm a simple shepherd."

"I think your right in some way," answered Harold. "War definitely takes place in the deepest, gloomiest twilight. I've been thinking about the Bavianer and what to do about them. A clear policy isn't so easy to see. They're always a threat, and their numbers don't seem to drop in any way. I wonder if we could train some Bavianer to fight against other Bavianer. You know, divide and rule until they are small enough in number for us to be safe."

"That could be an idea," answered Murdo. He poured another glass of ale from the pitcher.

Harold continued, "I think too that the big threat isn't the Bavianer themselves. It is the official religious sympathy for them. That could be the real danger—an ideology that holds that the Bavianer are an eternally put-upon and inferior sort of creature can be used by every priest as a prop to condemn others. When the settlement upriver is built, there will be more Bavianer fighting, and the Santa Fe school of thought in the Ancient Faith will use that fighting to gain advantage over the practical Hattusa ideas. Also, sympathy for the Bavianer by humans of the Ancient Faith sets up a sort of 'human status' competition."

"Whatever do you mean?" asked Murdo

"The Bavianer," said Harold, "are clearly inferior to us. You can't help but see that the instant you meet them, but at the same time, they are adapted to this moon and very dangerous. No Bavianer threatens those in the walled centers of the two downriver towns, and to live there, one must be pretty rich. They do threaten the working people upriver and outside town. By declaring them worthy of protection, one automatically shows how rich he or she is. Bavianer support is great for snob appeal."

"I suppose it is," answered Murdo. "I wonder how long that snob appeal will last. After all, snobbishness is based on fashion, and nothing changes faster than fashion."

"Do you know what happened to Yetzra?" asked Harold.

"You mean the priest who killed Greamand?" answered Murdo.

"Yes," answered Harold.

"I haven't seen him. I think he was sent away to Aviabron on mission work. The political situation in Santa Fe is much more unstable now than before, with the 'secularists' led by the Shepherds Guild pushing for reform and the 'saints' led by the high priestess pushing back. In Santa Fe, that situation is now called the Culture War. The news channels broadcast the controversy every night, and there have been fights in the street."

The pitcher was empty. Murdo had drunk more of the beer than Harold. He stood up in a wobbly way. "Well, I'm off to get my dogs and do what I needed to do. I'll be taking the sheep back to Santa Fe and need to get a move on to a nice stop over hill in between Santa Fe and Hattusa."

The two men shook hands and went their separate ways.

Harold went by the livery stable. He now had an extra camel to lead home, a minor inconvenience. Suddenly, from the sky, which was still light, Harold heard a hum. It was a Zeppelin. The craft was coming in low and slow and was brilliant with the reflected light from Boreas and the sun. The Zeppelin was making its Orbweekly journey in from

New Lydia. *Oh, had we had this service a year ago*, thought Harold. *The terrible siege might not have happened.*

The great craft slowly landed on the field. Passengers disembarked, and among them, wearing a felt dress, was Leyla. She was walking down the ramp.

She was beautiful.

Printed i
By Bool